GRACE AFTER THE RAIN

A Christian Romance Novel

Taretha Jones

Grace After the Rain

DEDICATION

I'd like to thank first and foremost, God. Without HIM I
would not have had the courage and drive to complete this
work.
I'd like to thank my parents, who taught me the value of
reading and writing, at an early age.
I would also like to thank the remainder of my family for their
love and support.
To my beautiful readers out there, thank you for reading this
book. I really do hope you enjoy it and are blessed in some
way by it.

THE STORYLINE

Thirty-something, Shawntriece, is a well-paid executive at a Fortune 500 corporation. Her life is practically perfect — at least to her it is. She has a beautiful home, an expensive car, a family who loves her, and two adorable twin daughters to cherish and spoil. However, despite everything that she has in the material world, she's sorely lacking in the spiritual realm. When life throws her a curve ball, will it end up being the chance she needs to find her way back to Christ? Will the relationship she develops with a saved, good-looking, single father grow into much more? Somehow, some way...will Shawntriece snatch herself a piece of grace after the rain that has fallen in her life?

Grace After the Rain

CHAPTER NUMBER ONE

Thirty-four-year-old, Shawntriece Avery sat down at her kitchen table and rubbed her temples with her forefingers. The simple massaging motion normally relaxed her. But not today. Today all she could think about was the problems in her life.

She rubbed her temples once again then let out a breath in a sigh. "Might as well go ahead and do it," she whispered under her breath as she picked up her cell phone and speed-dialed her attorney's office. After making it through the computerized introductory prompts, she finally got a live voice on the line.

"You've reached the office of Attorney James Eagleton. This is Marie. How can we help you today?"

"Marie…this is Shawntriece Avery. Could you transfer me to Mr. Eagleton, please?"

"Ah…Ms. Avery. Mr. Eagleton has a client in his office right now. Do you want me to leave him a message, asking him to call you, or would you rather I connect you to his voicemail?"

Shawntriece had nothing against modern-day technology. But at heart, she was an old-fashioned type of sista. So, she opted for having the attorney give her a return phone call. She wrapped up her conversation with the receptionist and placed her iPhone on the kitchen table in front of her. She shook her head and frowned.

"This is crazy," she whispered under her breath as she picked up the newspaper that was lying discarded on the kitchen table. The headline seemed to glare at her as she read it for what felt like the millionth time: *Local Vice President of Shugartsen Enterprises May Be Implicated Next…*

Right below the headline was a picture of Shawntriece, holding her hand up, trying to hide herself from the flash of some pseudo-paparazzi's camera.

She shook her head and flipped the newspaper over so she wouldn't have to see the imagery any longer. But not before she twisted her lips at the irony of the outfit she'd been wearing the day the picture had been taken. She'd been walking out the front doors of the ten-story, downtown building that had housed her former place of employment; paparazzi had jumped from behind a bush, surprising her.

The black and white, striped business suit had been one of her favorites. The Armani ensemble had cost her close to a grand. She wasn't used to dropping that much on clothing, but she'd felt like she deserved some type of reward when she'd been promoted to vice-president at Shugartsen almost three years ago — with the six-figure salary that came along with the promotion, she'd known she could afford it.

She drew her eyebrows together in a deeper frown. All she could think about right now was just how much the black and white ensemble reminded her of the prison jumpsuits she'd always seen in the movies.

Worried, she shook her head. "Up until that day, I hadn't worn that suit in months — in fact, the cleaners thought they'd lost it. Me wearing that suit when that picture was snapped… I bet it's a danggone sign. A sign that my butt's about to go to jail."

Jail. Prison. Lockdown.

Shawntriece felt beads of sweat starting to form on her forehead as she imagined what her life would be like if she somehow got caught up in the Ponzi scheme debacle that the CEO of her previous place of employment was going down for. She knew that professional news analysts had just announced a dire forecast for her ex-boss, Andrew Shagartsen. She knew they were whispering he was going to get at least 25 years. From her own research, she knew if she were tried and convicted for a supporting role in Andrew's crime, she'd be facing at least half that amount of time.

12 to 13 years. Her mind began processing images of all the things she would miss out on while sitting somewhere in a jail cell. The way it would affect the people in her life. Her family.

She normally had a very cool head. She wasn't the type of person who often catered to feeling panicky. But she suddenly felt as if the walls of her house were closing in on her. She could literally feel cold fingers of fear begin to tighten around her body.

Dingdong. Dingdong.

The melodic sound of her doorbell somehow provided a welcome reprieve from the emotions and sensations she was feeling.

Mama, she said in her head, knowing who was visiting her that morning. After all, her mother had told her last night that she had plans to drop by, bearing a stick-to-your-ribs type of breakfast. According to sixty-something Janice Avery, her little girl hadn't been eating properly lately and she was going to do something about it.

Shawntriece frowned as she made her way to her front door. With all the worrying she'd been doing recently — and because of the gravity of the offence she was possibly facing — Shawntriece didn't think that even the love of a doting and committed parent could lift her out of the state of despair she seemed to be falling into.

And not to mention Jesus. She twisted her lips. *I know mama's gonna try to feed me her spiel about how Jesus, God, and His whole host of heavenly angels can bring me out of this situation.*

She rolled her eyes. She didn't want to hear it.

However, needing a healthy dose of mama-love, she opened her front door anyway.

Janice Avery had concern in her eyes, even before she got one good look at her daughter. "Lord, Jesus," she said under her breath, shaking her head the whole while. "I can see the worry all over you, Shawny."

Yep, hearing her mother call her by her pet name immediately had a soothing effect on Shawntriece. It was something about her mother's soft, compassionate voice. It felt like a warm glass of milk before bedtime. A cozy blanket in winter… It was all love.

Janice tsked. "Let me put down this picnic basket so I can give my baby a hug."

Janice proceeded to wrap her comforting arms around her child and immediately began praying. "Father God, you know my baby ain't have nothing to do with that mess that went down over there at her job. I'm calling on you to be a hedge of protection around her. Give her peace in the storm, as only you know how to do…"

Shawntriece had been raised in the church, so she was familiar with the saints praying in such a fashion. A long time ago, she would've been praying right along with her mother. But life had happened and tarnished her relationship with God. She didn't consider herself to be a believer anymore. But at this moment in time, a small part of herself was following along with her mother's prayer.

When her mother said "Amen", Shawntriece almost opened her lips and whispered the same… Almost. She couldn't bring herself to do it.

Janice knew that her daughter was conflicted in her relationship with the Lord. But she had faith enough to believe that God would bring her child back into the fold. Accordingly, she smiled and placed a hand gently against her Shawntriece's cheek and said, "God'll do it, baby He'll work out the situation at your job."

An hour later, Shawntriece had a belly full of one of her favorite meals — her mother's breakfast casserole. Once again, she was sitting at her kitchen table alone, but she felt somewhat better about the charges that were possibly pending against her. She had a small amount of hope.

* * *

Across Town:

Janice was the mother of three children — all three of them daughters who weren't but a few years apart in age. Her girls had grown up doing everything together, which had led to them forming an unbreakable bond of sisterhood. Given their connection, Janice wasn't surprised that her other two girls — who were both currently out of town on business — had called her that morning, checking on Shawntriece. The only reason they hadn't called their sibling directly is that they both understood that Shawntriece preferred her personal space when dealing with certain life problems. Accordingly, Janice's youngest and oldest daughters, RoShonda and Angelica respectively, were doing their best to respect Shawntriece's need for privacy. Janice, on the other hand, ignored all of that. She rarely ever missed an opportunity to dole out her motherly love — especially when in her heart of hearts, she knew that her child really needed it.

As she stepped out of her car and made her way into the gym that the ladies from her church used for their physical fitness workouts, Janice still had thoughts of Shawntriece's situation on her mind. So much so that she almost tripped on her own two feet when she heard Celestine Miller saying something right behind her — it was on account of her being startled.

Falling into step with Janice, Celestine tucked a wayward gray strand under her colorful headband, chuckled then said, "I ain't scare you, did I, Janice?" Without waiting for a response, she added, "I said *hey* and waved. I thought you saw me."

Janice frowned at her friend of almost forty years. "You ought not sneak up on a body like that, Celestine. You darn near gave me a heart attack. What you tryna do… Send me to an early grave?" she grumbled.

"I was sure you heard me park my car a row behind yours… You always say you can hear my Mustang's engine from a mile away."

Ever since they'd been in their twenties, Celestine had had a love for vehicles with powerful engines. Normally, she would've made some type of lighthearted joke about her car, but noticing the look on her friend's face, she changed her mind. Instead, with a genuine look of concern in her eyes she said, "You went to see Shawntriece this morning, and you worried about her, ain't you?"

Janice let out a breath in a tired sounding sigh. She shook her head. "I ain't worried…cause I know God's got my baby's back. But I sure hate seeing her down like she is."

Celestine immediately gave her friend's arm a squeeze of encouragement. "Shawny's gonna be alright, Janice. You and me both been praying for her something fierce. And she's one strong Black woman…" She grinned. "Just like her momma—," she winked her eye, "—and her honorary Auntie Celestine."

Hearing her friend's words, Janice finally began to curl her lips upward in a smile, too. She knew her daughter would come out of her situation just fine, but it sure felt comforting hearing somebody else say it. She felt a warmth in her heart as she thought to herself: *Having a friend like Celestine is priceless.*

* * *

A Half Hour Later:

Still at home, Shawntriece picked up her cellphone as it began ringing. The caller ID panel on the device's face showed that it was her attorney's office getting back with her. She couldn't help but be nervous as her finger swiped the screen to accept the call. How could she not be? The rest of her life could be riding on what her attorney was about to tell her.

"This is Shawntriece—"

"Good morning, Ms. Avery. This is James Eagleton. And boy oh boy have I got some good news for you…"

Less than five minutes later, Shawntriece was disconnecting her call with tears of relief in her eyes. Mr. Eagleton was good friends with some higher-ups in the D.A.'s office. Because of his connections, he had inside knowledge on her case — that knowledge being that there would be no charges filed against her.

Since Shawntriece was a vice president at Shugartsen, it could've easily been assumed that she was somehow involved in the executive crimes that had been committed there — even though she'd vehemently declared her innocence. Surprisingly, the D.A. had chosen to lean in Shawntriece's favor. According to Shawntriece's attorney, the D.A. didn't want to waste the taxpayer's money on trying to implicate someone that they had virtually no evidence against.

Seconds after thanking Mr. Eagleton and disconnecting their phone call, Shawntriece began replaying her attorney's sweet words in her head: *"They already have the big fish in the pan — the CEO of Shugartsen. They're leaving it at that. You're free to move on with your life and career. You don't have to worry about this anymore, Ms. Avery."*

"They're leaving it at that! They're leaving it at that!" Shawntriece shouted as she began jumping up and down in joy in her kitchen.

She was the single mother of six-year-old twin girls, so the tears of happiness really began to flow as she thought about her kids. "Mama's not going to jail, babies," she whispered under her breath, as her tears of joy changed to tears of relief.

Then the burden of the entire situation finally hit her. She crumpled to the floor and really bawled for a good five minutes, as every emotion she'd been feeling for the last month or so washed over her.

For her kids' sake, she'd been keeping it all in…all together. But now that the danger was over with, she was finally having a breakdown and letting it all out.

CHAPTER NUMBER TWO

"Rise and shine, babies! It's time to get ready for school."

Shawntriece couldn't help but grin as she popped her head into her daughters' bedroom. Both girls were already jumping out of bed and pulling off their sleep bonnets.

"We up already, mommy," said Sierra, her toothy grin contagious.

"Yep," Bria immediately agreed.

Ever since the charges had been filed against her boss a couple of months ago, Shawntriece hadn't been her usual bubbly self with her girls. She'd tried to be upbeat. She'd tried to hide her problems and not let her depressed feelings get the better of her. But she was sure her worry had made an appearance in little ways. With James Eagleton's call yesterday, her concerns had vanished like smoke. She now felt as if she were free to give her kids a hundred percent of herself again, unadulterated. She felt like she could go back to actually being the type of mom she always strived to be. And yep, it sure felt good.

Shawntriece chuckled. "Alright, little ladies. Make your beds and meet me in the kitchen. We got thirty minutes to make it to school on time."

* * *

Exactly twenty-five minutes later, Shawntriece's BMW was slowly inching along in the caravan of parent vehicles. She was patiently awaiting her turn to drop her kids off at the front door of the private school they attended.

"Bria…Sierra…we're up next. Get ready to take off your seatbelts."

"Yes, ma'am," both girls responded, excited about the upcoming school day.

It was customary for the school to have teachers or members of its administration outside helping each student get out of their parent's vehicle. Today, the principal of the school approached Shawntriece's car.

With Principal Powell opening the back door of her car, letting her girls out, Shawntriece rolled down her passenger-side window and offered the man a friendly wave.

Calvary Powell smiled in return at all three of them. "Good morning, ladies," he said. "I'm looking forward to today being a good day at Higher Ground Academy." With a sparkle in them, his eyes met Shawntriece's. "I know Bria and Sierra probably told you about my little girl's birthday party weekend after next. I haven't received an RSVP back from you yet. But my Shanequa would really, really—," he smirked, "—did I say really?" A chuckle, "—be disappointed if the twins were a no-show." He grinned. "They're becoming besties in class, you know."

With all the problems Shawntriece had been facing lately at her job, the invitation to the birthday party had totally escaped her mind.

"Yeah, mama," the twins said, almost in unison. "Can we go? Pleeeeeease…"

With a look of embarrassment painting her face, Shawntriece looked at her girls and nodded her head. "Of course, you can go, you guys. Tell you the truth, Mama almost forgot all about it. I'm sorry about that."

As Bria and Sierra both jumped for joy, Shawntriece focused her attention back on Mr. Powell. "It's gonna be at two o'clock at the Chuck E. Cheese on Friendly Avenue, right?"

He grinned again. "Yep, you got it."

"Alright. We'll be there."

Not wanting to hold up the line any longer, Shawntriece waved goodbye to her girls as Mr. Powell walked Bria and Sierra to the entrance doors of the school. She began making her way from the facility and going about her day.

She frowned to herself as she turned out the premises and onto the city street. *Since I'm jobless with time to kill, guess I'll make my way to Starbucks and treat myself to a Frappuccino. While I'm there, I might as well relax, go online and see if I can find any job leads.*

Dropping her kids off at school was a normal task that Shawntriece undertook — she'd been performing the chore ever since she'd started her babies at Higher Ground Academy a year ago. However, turning right onto Market Street instead of turning left and heading downtown to the business district, that part was unusual for her. It had been almost a month since Shawntriece had last stepped into the high-rise building that housed

Shugartsen Enterprises, and she was really beginning to miss her job.

But something's gonna jump off for me in the job arena. I'm talented… Well qualified. It's only gonna be a matter of time.

Minutes later, she was parking her BMW and making her way into her favorite downtown coffee shop. She'd just placed her order and had sat down when a brown-skinned sista with a vaguely familiar face said, "You're the twins' mom, right?"

The moment that comment moved past the friendly-looking woman's lips, Shawntriece remembered where she'd seen her face before. *Higher Ground Academy. She drops off the little girl with the locs. She's a parent at my babies' school.*

Shawntriece offered up a friendly smile. "Yes, I'm Sierra and Bria's mom. I've seen you in line at Higher Ground. Your little girl...she's in Ms. Donovan's class, too. Right?"

The woman extended her palm towards Shawntriece for a handshake. "Yep. I'm Jasmine Hunter. My daughter's name is Imani. Nice to meet you."

Shawntriece shook the hand being offered and smiled again. "Shawntriece Avery. And nice to meet you, too."

"I'm taking Imani to Mr. Powell's birthday party for his little girl weekend after next. Bria and Sierra coming?"

Shawntriece nodded her head. "Yep, I'm gonna make sure they make it there." She laughed. "My girls and Mr. Powell got on me about it this morning. I haven't sent my RSVP back in yet. It kinda slipped my mind."

Jasmine giggled. "I feel you on that. My Imani made sure I handed that thing to Mr. Powell a couple weeks ago. And speaking of Mr. Powell… He sure is a fine hunk of chocolate, ain't he, girlfriend?"

Given that she'd given up on men a long time ago, noticing whether or not Mr. Powell was a hunk of chocolate hadn't made it across Shawntriece's mind. Well, actually it had — the man was a good-looking brotha — but she'd chosen to ignore it.

Not noticing her conversation partner's disinterest, Jasmine continued speaking. "Almost all the single ladies bringing their kids to Higher Ground trying to snag brotha man. He's single and unattached, you know. On top of that, he's a good dad."

After dropping that line, Jasmine suddenly and finally read the look on Shawntriece's face. "Oh," she said, slightly embarrassed. "My bad." She laughed. "I can tell you ain't even interested. You must be lucky enough to have a significant other." She frowned. "Unlike myself and half the women I know."

Shawntriece had technically just met Jasmine. So, she wasn't going there with her. She wasn't about to discuss the somewhat intimate details of her life with a virtual stranger.

"Well," Jasmine said. "It was nice chit-chatting with you this morning, Shawntriece. I'm due at my job in a little under an hour. Guess I'll see you in line at Higher Ground."

Shawntriece nodded. "Yeah… See you around, Jasmine."

Two hours later, Shawntriece finally closed her laptop and made her way out of Starbucks. She'd only found two job openings that seemed like they would fit the bill for her skill set. However, she felt confident in her ability to snag both positions. *My master's degree and experience at Shugartsen as a VP are gonna work in my favor.*

She smiled to herself. "I'll be back in the job world before I know it."

CHAPTER NUMBER THREE

"Well, big sis… How's the job search going?"

How's the job search going? That was the one question Shawntriece didn't feel like being asked right now. She'd thought for sure she would've received a call back in reference to her job applications. But nothing had happened yet. Nada. Zilch. In fact, a follow-up call to one of her prospective employers had revealed that the company had already filled the open position with a candidate that wasn't her. As for the other few job openings she'd applied to, crickets.

Shawntriece grimaced, causing her sister, RoShonda, to do the same. "That bad, huh?"

Shawntriece nodded her head. "Yeah, that bad."

"Well, you only been looking for what? Five or six weeks? I read the other day — in my Black Enterprise Magazine that came in the mail — that when a person's trying to get an executive position, it can take months for something to come through." She gave her sibling's arm a squeeze of encouragement. "So, don't give up hope. And you know we all praying for you."

"Right. Praying for me."

RoShonda held in her grimace. She wanted to say something to her older sibling about the power of God and all his goodness, but they'd been down that road before. Too many times.

Shawntriece, however, didn't hold in her frown. She shook her head and shared, "I know what you over there thinking, Shonda."

RoShonda shrugged her shoulders. "I ain't saying nothing, Shawny. You've made your position clear...a whole lotta times. E'rybody who knows you knows how you feel about God and religion."

"Okay." Shawntriece took a tiny sip from her bottle of water. "Well, thanks for recognizing that." In a tiny act of concession — in the spirit of sisterhood and getting along — she also added, "And thanks for having positive thoughts about my situation and sending positive energy my way… I appreciate it."

"You're welcome." Shonda smiled. "You're my sister and I love you, girl."

Shawntriece twisted her lips in a wry-looking, quirky little line. "Even though I'mma backsliding heathen?"

Backsliding heathen. Those were words that some of the mothers of their childhood church home had used to describe Shawntriece on the hush-hush. Behind closed doors. However, they were words that RoShonda had never used in reference to her sibling. RoShonda had chosen to take the approach of praying for her sister, instead. RoShonda prayed that God would step in and open up Shawntriece's heart.

"We all sin and fall short of God's glory from time to time, sis. Like Grandma used to say: *We all one misdeed or two from being off the straight path.*" RoShonda smiled. "Now, with that being said, let me stop stuffing my face and head over to the grocery store. Brayden's birthday is tomorrow. He loves homemade yellow cake. Homemade oxtails and rice, too. I'mma surprise my man with a special dinner… Even though you know I hate cooking oxtails." She playfully shriveled up her face in disgust. "I hate the feel of them thangs in my hands when I'm washing 'em. And the name's not good…as far as imagery's concerned. Know what I mean?"

Brayden was RoShonda's boyfriend of a few months. Being a single mom to her two girls, with no man in sight and seeing no need for one, Shawntriece couldn't imagine herself going out her way to prepare a special meal that she herself hated cooking. However, in the name of keeping the peace, she wasn't about to share any of that with her sibling. She simply nodded her head and said, "Because my little sister can burn in the kitchen, I'm sure you're gonna do an excellent job on the meal. And I'm doubly sure he's gonna like it. So, stop worrying. Now, on a different but connected subject… Don't stay up too late with your boo. That birthday party that we're taking Bria and Sierra to starts at noon tomorrow. I'll be swinging by your place at eleven-thirty to pick you up."

"Don't worry. I'll be ready, Shawny."

"Thanks, Shonda. I know I've said it before, but I'm really glad that you like having such an active role in your nieces' lives. They love them some Auntie Shonda… And I love you, too."

"The love goes both ways, sis."

RoShonda threw her sibling a parting grin as she walked out of Shawntriece's home and into the bright sunshine. However, as the door closed behind her, she couldn't help but think: *Yep, I definitely love my sister and her kids; I'll always be there for them whenever they need me. But Lord knows I wish them babies had a daddy in their life. Shawntriece is a great mom, but I think my nieces feel like they're still missing out. And I don't know how long me trying to step in and fill a pseudo-daddy role is gonna work.*

Prompted by her thoughts, RoShonda said another quick prayer for her sister and her little family.

* * *

Across Town:

"Hey Cal, what you and my favorite niece up to?"

Calvary grinned as soon as his sister walked through his front door. "Well, you just missed Shanequa. Mama came and swooped her up and they're heading to the mall for a mani/pedi." He chuckled. "I think that's what you ladies call it."

"Yeah. I remember mama said she was gonna do that with Neek one day soon. I guess it's a pre-birthday gift of sorts."

Calvary nodded. "Yep. If I remember correctly, those were mama's exact words." While saying that, Calvary couldn't help but think to himself: *Things like that… As a single Dad, that's why I'm glad I have Mom and my little sister in my daughter's life.*

He grinned, causing Yolanda to laugh and say, "A'ight, a'ight, bro. I bet you over there imagining how ridiculous you'd look if you were the one at the spa getting your nails painted light pink with Shanequa." She held a hand in front of herself, casually inspecting her own vibrant fuchsia nails. "You know light pink or clear were the only colors mama let me get when I was Shanequa's age. Mama believed in little girls having fun, but not acting grown."

Calvary chuckled.

"Well anyhootie," she said. "What you up to now that you got the house to yourself for a minute?"

He pointed towards his laptop that was on the coffee table in the center of the living room.

"Work," she stated.

He smiled. "Busted. How'd you know?"

"I just know you, big brother." She winked her eye. Although, the carrot sticks are a big hint. Back when we were kids and in school, you were always chewing on carrot sticks whenever you were serious about your homework." She laughed. "Grandma Pauline used to say you were the most health-conscious child she ever laid eyes on. Remember?"

Fond memories of his late grandmother quickly danced through Calvary's mind. "Indeed, I do, sis."

"Well, are you working on the budget or something else?" She smiled. "You know I can always look over your numbers for you."

His sister was an accountant by profession. So, Calvary knew she was exceptionally talented in the mathematics arena. However, number crunching wasn't his problem today.

"Actually, sis. I'm going over applications for the assistant principal position."

Yolanda made her way over to a side chair in the room and sat down. "Oh, so you've narrowed it down to a lucky candidate or two and you can't make up your mind on your final decision."

"Um, not really."

She raised an eyebrow and in response, Calvary continued speaking. "The person that I want to offer the job to hasn't even submitted an application. In fact, she probably doesn't even know about the position."

Thinking that she understood, Yolanda nodded her head. "So, you're trying to get a superstar on your team. A hotshot in the field of academia. One of the PhD people in one of those journals you like to read."

Calvary shook his head. "No. I actually wanna offer the job to one of the parents."

"Parents? As in parent of one of the kids who go to Higher Ground?"

"Yep."

Calvary knew it would probably sound ridiculous to someone who wasn't a person of faith. However, his sister took her relationship with God seriously. So, he figured she'd understand what he was about to say.

He looked his sibling in the eye and said, "I was greeting the parents during drop off a few days ago — like usual — and the minute I laid eyes on one of the parents, God put a message on my heart. He told me: *Give her the job*." He paused and added, "And before you say anything…no, I don't know her qualifications. I just know that God told me to offer her the position. I even had a follow-up dream about it last night."

Knowing her brother, Yolanda replied, "Ah ha... So, before I showed up at your front door, you were on your laptop googling her."

"Indeed, I was, sister dear."

"Okay. So, what did you find? What did Mr. Internet tell you? She in school administration or nah?"

Calvary sat down on the sofa with his laptop on the coffee table in front of him. He looked at the professional profile page that he'd pulled up on Shawntriece Avery from an employment talent website.

"Well, she hasn't worked in school administration — she's worked in the corporate arena. She has two bachelor's degrees… One in business and administration, the other in education. She has a master's in business. Until recently, she was an executive at Shugartsen Enterprises."

Shugartsen Enterprises… Why does that name sound familiar? That's the question that suddenly popped up in Yolanda's head.

As if reading his sister's mind, Calvary said, "Shugartsen… It's the corporation that's been in the local news lately. There was some corruption… You know, amongst the higher ups—"

A lightbulb went off in Yolanda's head. Without allowing her brother to finish his spiel, she interrupted with, "And this person you're looking to hire, she was one of them. One of the fallen stars. One of those execs."

Yolanda snapped her fingers. "I bet she's the gorgeous sista that News 2 said the feds are thinking about investigating."

Calvary was a widow of almost six years. Ever since his wife's death, he'd trained himself not to really notice if a female was gorgeous or not, so he hadn't really been looking at Shawntriece in that way. But now that he got to thinking about it, he had to admit that the mother of two had a pretty smile and was easy on the eyes.

Wearing a slightly dubious expression on her face, Yolanda asked, "She's the one?"

"Yep. She's probably the one you're talking about. But before you go there…I did some digging and all signs point to her not being guilty of anything. In fact, the prosecutors aren't going after her. They announced it on the news a few weeks ago." He smiled. "Plus, she volunteered at the school for some of our functions. It never crossed my mind to think that she has a deceitful bone in her body. She seems like the type of person who's always giving…not taking." He smiled even harder. "And on top of that, her twin girls are becoming Neek's best friends. So…"

Yolanda nodded her head in understanding. "She gets triple votes of approval. One from you. One from my niecey-poo. And most of all—," she pointed a single finger upwards, "—one from the Man upstairs."

He laughed. "Pretty much."

Yolanda smiled. "So, I guess you need to go ahead and offer her the job that she hasn't even applied for. And that you don't know whether or not she'll turn down." She paused for a moment and warned, "You know she probably got a line of companies waiting to hire her, right?"

"Yeah. I figured so. But God keeps telling me to offer her the position. So, you know how your big bro likes to roll…"

"Yep. When the Master says move, you try to be obedient. That's one of the things I like about you, Calvary." She paused for a few seconds and asked, "So when you gonna reach out to her about the position? How?"

Deep in thought, he pinched his chin between his thumb and forefinger a couple of times. "Well, she's bringing her girls to Neek's birthday party tomorrow. I believe I'll pull her to the side and talk to her while we're there."

Yolanda nodded her head. "Um, okay. That sounds like a solid plan to me."

He smiled. "Glad you think so, sis."

CHAPTER NUMBER FOUR

Shawntriece pulled her car into an empty slot in the crowded parking lot outside of their local Chuck E. Cheese. It was early October, but the thermometer was reading temps that were typical of a sunny summer day…eighty-three degrees. And the perfectly blue skies were right in line with the temps.

Sitting in the passenger seat of Shawntriece's ride, RoShonda glanced over at her sibling and said, "I bet if Principal Powell had known today was gonna be so pretty, he would've had the party outside somewhere. Girl, today's feeling like the middle of July."

Over the excited conversation that her daughters were having in the backseat of the car, Shawntriece barely made out what her sister had just said. "Yep, you're right, Shonda." She laughed as she looked over her shoulder at her girls. "Now let's get these two inside before they bounce out the dang-gone sunroof."

RoShonda chuckled, too. "Right."

Less than two minutes later, the four were walking through the front doors of the play place, two gifts in tow, one from each twin for the birthday girl. Per security procedure at the establishment, a Chuck E. Cheese's employee stamped all members of their little group's hands. Then excited, Bria and Sierra made a beeline for the long table at which their bestie's party was being hosted. Shawntriece and RoShonda followed at a much slower pace.

Before they reached their destination, RoShonda leaned into Shawntriece's ear and said, "It looks like only a handful of the parents are staying. Most of them done dropped their kids off and bounced. Maybe we should do the same and come back in a couple of hours. You trust Mr. Powell, right?" She laughed. "He *is* the principal of Sierra and Bria's school—," she glanced around, "—and y'all got all these chaperones in here. Not to mention the Chuck E. Cheese's staff…they all about security."

Shawntriece frowned inwardly. Yep, the staff was all about security, and it was true that Principal Powell was responsible for her girls 8am to 2pm most days of the week. But she didn't trust leaving her babies without herself — or a trusted family member — in a situation like this. Shawntriece was too much of a helicopter parent for that.

"Nah?" RoShonda knowingly asked.

Shawntriece shook her head. "Nope. But I'll be okay if you wanna leave. You can take the Beemer and come back for us in a couple of hours."

"I'm good, sis. You, me, and the twins came here as a package. And that's how we're leaving." She winked her eye and laughed. "Plus, I know how you hate being by yourself in social settings like this. Let's go greet the host and mingle."

A few seconds later, Shawntriece was smiling at Principal Powell and saying over the cacophony of happy voices, "It looks like Shanequa's gonna have a ball today."

Pleased with the party's turnout, Calvary nodded his head and grinned right back at the mother of his daughter's best friends. "Yep. I somehow managed to pull it off."

A pretty woman — who Shawntriece assumed to be Principal Powell's girlfriend for some reason — playfully elbowed him in the side and laughed. "You definitely managed to pull it all off… With a whole lotta help. And I do mean a *whooole* lot," she emphasized.

The woman extended her hand. "You must be Bria and Sierra's mom and auntie. According to the birthday girl — my niece — her besties' momma and Auntie Shonda were bringing them to the party."

Shawntriece shook the hand that the woman offered. "That would be us. I'm Shawntriece… Bria and Sierra's mom—," she nodded her head to acknowledge her sibling, "—and this is my sister, RoShonda."

"Nice to finally meet you guys. I'm Principal Powell's sister, Yolanda."

Yolanda surprised the little group by turning to her brother and saying, "I'll keep an eye on things in here for a few minutes so you can talk to Shawntriece in private, bro. I recommend going outside where it's a lot quieter."

Talk to me in private? What in the world about? I know both my girls have been doing well in school so far this year.

Her experience in business negotiations allowed Shawntriece to hide the look of surprise that wanted to show itself on her face.

Principal Powell's eyes met Shawntriece's. He smiled again. "I wouldn't have necessarily led into needing to talk to you like that, Ms. Avery. But can I talk to you outside for a few minutes?"

Beyond curious, Shawntriece swiped her hand towards the front of the restaurant in a gracious manner. "Sure… Lead the way, Mr. Powell."

Less than a minute later, Shawntriece drew her eyebrows together in confusion and said, "Excuse me… Come again?"

Understanding her surprise, the principal nodded his head and repeated, "I'd like to offer you the position of assistant principal at Higher Ground Academy."

"Uh… You do?"

"Yes, I do."

"Not to sound disrespectful, but why would you want to offer me the position? I haven't applied for it. And you don't even know if I'm qualified."

"Well, I'm a man of faith, Ms. Avery. God put it on my heart to offer the position. So that's what I'm doing."

Wow, this is crazy. A sista can't catch a break from the holy rollies and their acts of belief and faith. My mama, my sisters, and now the principal of my kids' school. She fought the urge to roll her eyes. *But I guess it comes with the territory when you send your child to a faith-based, private school. My butt shouldn't even be surprised.*

Her eyes finally met his. "I actually double majored in college…business and education. I have a Bachelors in both, and a Master's in business. I taught 6th grade during the day and worked on my master's degree in the evenings. So, I guess in an odd type of way, I kinda might be qualified for the position—"

"But you're not interested," he interrupted. He slowly curled his lips upward. "You enjoy running with the big dogs in the private sector."

She matched his grin with a tiny one of her own. "Right. Seems like you have me figured out."

He nodded. "I understand. Like I said, God put it on my heart to ask, so, that's what I did." He grabbed the handle to the front door of the building. "Now… If it's okay with you, let's get back inside and join the festivities. Although I'm sure the girls aren't really missing us." He chuckled. "My guess is they're too busy having fun."

As Shawntriece walked through the open door that Principal Powell held open for her, she looked over her shoulder, then agreeing she added, "I'm sure they are."

Shawntriece made a beeline to where her sister was standing playing a version of Whack-a-Mole with the twins and several other kids.

RoShonda took a step back from the throng with a quickness and leaned into her sister's ear. "Girl, is everything alright?" she asked, low-key trying to be secretive by keeping her voice down.

"Yep," Shawntriece replied.

"Well, what did he say?" RoShonda said, her voice still low in volume.

Sometimes I think my little sister has no tact at all, Shawntriece thought to herself as she tried to use her eyes to nonverbally communicate to RoShonda that now wasn't the time for talking.

Finally catching on, RoShonda formed her mouth into an "o" shape and turned her lips up in a tiny smile of embarrassment. "We'll talk later on today… Like after we leave here and take the kids home."

"Yeah, later."

* * *

Four Hours Later:

RoShonda flopped herself down on her sibling's living room sofa and said, "Girl, I knew the minute we got the twins home, they were gonna need a nap."

Shawntriece let out a little chuckle. "Nah, honey…won't be no napping going on this evening. After all that running around at that party, they're out for the count. That's why I went ahead and gave them a bath and had them put on their pajamas. I know it's only a little past six, but your nieces aren't waking up 'til tomorrow morning… You can trust and believe that."

RoShonda grinned. "I feel you, sis. Now speaking of the party, what did Principal Powell call you outside for?" She sucked her teeth. "Giiiirl… You know a sista been burning up with curiosity ever since early this afternoon."

"He offered me a job."

Surprise instantly worked itself into RoShonda's eyes. "A job? You applied for a position at Bria and Sierra's school?"

"Nope."

"He just offered you a job out the blue?"

Shawntriece nodded her head. "Pretty much. He asked me to take on the role of assistant principal."

As much as she wanted to drop all the details of the conversation with Principal Powell, Shawntriece knew better than telling her sister about how the man had said God had instructed him to offer her the position. *I'll be opening up a big ol' can of worms if I go there.*

"Hmmm, that's odd," RoShonda said. Then she smiled, "But God *does* work in mysterious ways. When do you start? Monday?"

"I told him no."

"You told him no?" RoShonda asked in disbelief.

"Yep."

"I know it's not gonna pay six figures like your old gig. But you've been saying for years that you're tempted to go back into the education field. Seems like to me that now is as good a time as any… Especially since you have *zero* income coming in right now."

Shawntriece drew her eyebrows together in a frown. "You were just telling me the other day that God would bless me with a job comparable to the one at Shugartsen or better… Um, what happened to all that?"

Still managing to keep a good-hearted state of composure about herself, RoShonda rolled her eyes and smiled sweetly. "I never said it would be comparable from a financial standpoint. Maybe it's the job satisfaction area that you're about to be blessed in. Either way, if I were in your shoes, I'd take it. A job as an assistant principal is better than having no job at all. "Plus," she reasoned, "it'll align with Bria and Sierra's day. That'll make life a whole lot easier for you. I bet there'll be no more long hours of afterschool care for the girls. That'll save you almost a grand per month right there."

Shawntriece had to admit that her sibling had made a good point. But she still wasn't convinced that taking on the assistant principal position would be a good idea. She shared with her sister as much.

Hearing Shawntriece's rebuttal and the sound of a car pulling into the driveway, RoShonda stood up from the sofa she'd been lounging on. "Well, at the end of the day, it's your decision, sister dear. And on that note, that sounds like Brayden out in your driveway. We only have twenty minutes to make it to that specialty hardware store I was telling you about. I wanna show him those latches in person so I can get his opinion on 'em. Since he's an architect and all, he has an eye for things like that." She smiled. "He's been a blessing to have around for my remodeling project. Kisses, sis… Catch you later."

"Okay, hon."

As she locked the deadbolt on her front door and manned her home security system, Shawntriece let out a breath in a sigh. It had been a long day and she was tired.

With her daughters asleep, she now had the house all to herself. So, she decided to run a bubble bath and pamper herself a little bit.

Luxuriating in the warm oasis of fluffy, white bubbles, she began thinking over her day. Of course, her thoughts landed on the job proposition.

I'm unemployed right now — and I don't know where my next paycheck's coming from — but I know I made the right decision in turning that offer down. That's all there is to it.

CHAPTER NUMBER FIVE

Given her position on faith, Shawntriece made it a point to sleep in most Sundays. Spending time in the house of the Lord — like the vast majority of people in her immediate family — was a no-go for her. It was out of the question.

The weird thing: Shawntriece allowed her mother to take her girls to church from time to time, despite the fact that she had no interest in stepping in there herself.

Today was one such day. Janice Avery had picked up her twin granddaughters a half hour ago and now Shawntriece had the next four hours all to her lonesome.

She'd always had a thing for doing her own nails, so she decided to treat herself to a quickie manicure. Once she accomplished that task, she decided to head to the mall. Given her current state of joblessness, she figured that limiting her spending was the best course of action for right now. Hence, she knew that window shopping would be all she accomplished today at one of her favorite shopping complexes.

She was fingering a silk blouse in Macy's when she heard a familiar voice call her name.

"Shawntriece Avery… Is that you?"

Shawntriece turned around and flashed her former college professor, Dr. Diane Barnes, a warm, friendly smile. "Dr. Barnes… hi!"

Seeing that Dr. Barnes had been a mentor of sorts to Shawntriece, Shawntriece wasn't at all surprised that the woman gave her an affectionate hug in greeting.

Pulling back from their embrace, Dr. Barnes said, "I know you got my email of encouragement a few weeks ago, but I placed your name on my calendar to give you a call tomorrow. I wanted to check in on you… You know, see how things are going on the professional front."

Seeing the genuine concern in the woman's eyes, Shawntriece decided to confess. Grimacing, she said, "Things haven't been going too well lately, Dr. Barnes. Finding a new job has been a challenge." She shook her head. "More than a challenge really…it seems impossible."

"Aw, yes…I'm sure it's been a challenge, dear." A frowned marred the sixty-something's beautiful caramel-toned complexion. "I'm not being arrogant, but over the years, I've found that I'm a pretty good judge of character. So, I know you had nothing to do with that mess that went down at Shugartsen. It's been ages ago, but something similar happened to me back when I was around your age. My best advice to you is to step away from the business arena for a while — I reckon a year or so will do. You need to let the flames go down… Give people time to get their tongues wagging about some other bad situation that's bound to happen in the business community. It's unfortunate, but something's always happening in our field. Some con. Some hostile takeover. Some sort of scandal."

The woman smiled. "And once you let the flames go down — then like you young folks like to say — you'll be back on your 'A' game."

The two talked for a couple minutes more before going their separate ways. As Shawntriece placed the silk shirt she'd been holding during her conversation with Dr. Barnes back on the rack, she suddenly had a eureka moment.

The job offer that Principal Powell gave me… That would be the perfect opportunity for me to take Dr. Barnes' advice. That job will keep me out of the business arena for close to a year, while bringing in a decent salary. I won't have to deplete my savings, and when the flames die down — like Dr. Barnes said they would — I can search for a new job in the corporate sphere.

Dr. Barnes' confidence was contagious. Shawntriece had hope again. She finally knew the path she needed to take.

Part of Shawntriece wanted to wait until the following day — Monday — to contact Calvary Powell. Part of her wanted to flop down at one of the tables in the mall's food court and email the man right now. The latter part of herself won out. That's why her thumbs were flying over her cellphone, composing an email that read:

Mr. Powell, after much thought, I've changed my mind about accepting your administrative job offer. If the position is still open, I'd love to be an assistant principal at Higher Ground Academy. I've included my personal cell phone number in this message. I look forward to hearing from you soon. Thank you in advance, Shawntriece Avery.

Shawntriece's index finger hovered over the "send" icon for a few seconds as she inwardly asked herself: *Should I really be doing this?*

Then Dr. Barnes' words came back into her head and she followed through with the mission.

She smiled. *That's it for that. Now the ball's in Principal Powell's court.*

* * *

Across Town:

Sitting at his mother's long dining room table, Calvary bowed his head in reverence and began to bless the Sunday dinner that his mother and sisters had prepared. Besides church service, in Calvary's eyes, this was one of the best parts of Sunday. The food was always excellent, but it was the fellowship of his large, affectionate family that he enjoyed most at Mamie Powell's ranch-style home. Any given Sunday, his mother and at least four out of six of her kids surrounded the long table. In the past seven years, the addition of three grandchildren had upped the headcount.

The family had finished eating their meal when Calvary's sister, Yolanda, asked him to carry a heavy double ottoman that their mother had gifted her out to her car.

Right after Calvary got the ottoman settled into the back of the SUV, Yolanda said, "Well, bro, I had to leave Shanequa's party early, so, I didn't get the chance to ask you about what went down when you talked to the twins' mama yesterday… She said no, didn't she?"

Calvary flexed his back muscles real quick, stretching after the exertion of handling the heavy piece of furniture. "Well," he smiled. "Yes and no."

"Huh?"

"She told me no yesterday at the party. But while we were eating Sunday dinner today, she shot me an email saying that she wanted to take me up on my offer. When I get home later on this afternoon, I'm gonna reply to her email and ask her if she can come over to the academy tomorrow morning — we need to get the formalities out the way." He grinned. "The school board's gonna say yes to me hiring her because they've already told me that they're leaving the decision of choosing a candidate up to me. But I'm pretty much sure they're gonna still want to see some official paperwork… The official completed job application, a background check and whatnot."

Catching the look on his sibling's face, Calvary chuckled. "You were sure she was gonna turn me down, huh, sis?"

Yolanda grinned. "I gotta admit I thought she was gonna say no. I'm pretty much sure homegirl's used to pulling in six figures…if not more. I can't imagine your school paying her anywhere close to that." She hmphed. "She'll be lucky to get half of what she's used to being paid. Although I gotta admit that half of a hundred grand is still decent money. I'll certainly take it." She laughed. "But since I don't have an MBA and a bachelor's in education, I'm also pretty much sure I'm not qualified. Either way, congratulations on filling the position… I know for darn sure that takes a burden off your mind."

"Indeed, it does, sis."

"Indeed, it does what?"

Both Calvary and Yolanda turned around when their youngest brother, twenty-five-year-old Xavier, walked towards them and posed his question.

"Well—," Yolanda said, "—our big brother here said that God told him to offer an assistant principal job to one of the parents at Higher Ground Academy… The twins' mom. You know, Shanequa's little friends."

Xavier slowly raised his lips in a sly-looking grin. "You mean the thick hottie in the purple jeans who was at Chuck E. Cheese's yesterday?"

Yolanda shook her head and rolled her eyes at the same time. Then she grinned and said, "Boy, that girl is at least ten years older than your young behind. Plus, I'm sure she wouldn't be interested in giving a playa like yourself the time of day. She's an ex-executive. A professional. She's raising two kids and I'm sure she ain't got no time for playing games. And she probably even married."

Xavier shook his head. "Nope. I didn't see a ring on her finger at Neek's party. A classy sista like herself would've had her bling on display if she was somebody's wifey."

He rubbed his hands together as if anticipating a tasty meal. Then he turned to Calvary and said, "You gonna introduce me to her, right, bruh?"

Calvary chuckled. "Nope. Her girls and Neek are good friends…almost besties. Your relationships tend to blow up in your face, creating havoc. Somehow, I think some of that havoc might rub off on Neek's relationship with Ms. Avery's girls." He chuckled again. "Plus, like

Yolanda said, Shawntriece Avery's out your league, youngblood."

Xavier grimaced, then raised his lips in a good-natured grin. "The two of y'all just playa hating on a brotha." He pulled his keys out his pocket. "But that's a'ight. There's plenty of fish in the sea." He winked an eye. "In fact, I'm about to go reel one in right now."

Yolanda laughed. Calvary did, too. "Our little brother's a mess. We're gonna have to pray a little harder for that one."

"Right," Yolanda agreed. "Well anyway, congratulations on filling the assistant principal position. Based on you saying that God told you to offer the job to Shawntriece Avery, I can't wait to see how it all plays out."

A look of contemplation ran across Calvary's face. Then he said, "Me, too, sis. Me, too."

CHAPTER NUMBER SIX

After pulling into the parking lot of Higher Ground Academy, Shawntriece headed towards the visitor parking area instead of the designated student drop off zone. Bria was the first of her twins to notice the difference in their regular Monday through Friday routine.

"Mama, you went the wrong way," Bria said, thinking her parent had made a mistake. The child pointed towards the side of the school. "You're supposed to drop us off right there… 'member?"

Principal Powell had offered her the assistant principal job, but since she didn't have an official contract, Shawntriece hadn't told her girls about the probability of her working at their school. Shawntriece's original plan had been to park and tell her twins that she had to talk to their principal about something, so, she would be accompanying them inside the building. However, Shawntriece now realized that taking that approach would lead to unnecessary discussions. *I gotta admit that my babies are inquisitive* — she frowned, then grinned — *more like nosy. They got that from their Auntie Shonda.*

Revising her plan, she smiled at her kids and cranked her engine back up. "Right. Silly ol' me. Mama's trippin' this morning." She laughed. "Sorry, girls. Let me drop you off."

Two minutes later, Bria and Sierra had disappeared into the building and Shawntriece was pulling back into the visitor's lot. She checked her appearance in the rearview mirror and took a deep breath.

Why am I nervous? she asked her reflection. *It's not like I'm going in there to interview for a vice president position or something. Plus, the man said I've already got the job.*

She shook her head and sighed. *After everything I've been through the past couple months, I guess it's just a case of latent reaction and nerves.*

Realizing that she was nine minutes away from her and Principal Powell's agreed upon meeting time, Shawntriece stepped out of her car and made her way inside the schoolhouse.

Less than five minutes later, she was walking into Principal Powell's office.

Calvary smiled in greeting. "Ms. Avery…good morning."

She smiled in return. "Good morning, Principal Powell."

He shook his head. "Principal Powell is too formal. *Mr.* Powell will do."

"Okay. *Mr.* Powell… Good morning."

"Again, good morning." Another smile.

The two stood there grinning at each other for several seconds, long enough for Shawntriece to think to herself: *All this smiling is getting a little awkward.*

Her former position in the executive world caused her to quickly scan her brain for a comment to break the awkwardness of the moment. However, Calvary beat her to the punch.

"Thank you for filling out the official job application online last night, Miss Avery. I know one of the emails I sent you contained a summary of the assistant principal position, but I'd like to answer any questions you may have. We can do that right now."

Shawntriece had compiled a list of eight specific questions and/or concerns. She'd placed that list in her briefcase and brought it with her that morning. Accordingly, she smiled at Calvary, popped open her briefcase and said, "Alright, since you mentioned it—"

He interrupted her with a chuckle — a laugh that Shawntriece realized she liked the sound of. "You came well prepared," he said. "That's a sign that I gave the job to the right person after all."

Shawntriece looked her new boss in the eye. "So, God told you to offer me the position, but you had doubts."

Just because he was a man of faith, it didn't mean that Calvary was perfect. Calvary understood that he had faults and fears, even though one of his favorite Bible verses was: *God hath not given us a spirit of fear, but a spirit of power and of love.*

Calvary had, indeed, began to fear that he'd somehow made a mistake in thinking God had told him to offer a job to the woman who was standing in front of him lowkey smirking.

Calvary nodded his head. "I'm only a man, Ms. Avery. I have to admit that I had a few doubts from time to time about this job offer situation." He smiled. "But each time the doubt would rear its ugly head, I'd tell myself to stop listening to the devil. I know I was supposed to offer you a job. It's not a coincidence that you're qualified for the position. And since I initially had no idea you had a degree in education, I tend to think all of this is part of God's plan."

Calvary Powell was Shawntriece's new boss, so she'd expected to walk into the school and immediately establish an ultra-professional type of relationship with the man. However, for some odd reason — one unknown to Shawntriece — she felt comfortable in Principal Powell's presence. It felt like he was an old friend. Accordingly, she chuckled and said, "*Initially…* You said *initially*. That makes me think you snooped around and somehow investigated me."

He laughed again and said, "Busted… I looked you up online on LinkedIn." He pointed at the piece of paper in her hand, "And on that note, let's address those questions that you have before I somehow put my foot in my mouth or get myself in trouble."

* * *

Later that Afternoon:

Shawntriece was in her new office going over the school's bylaws when Principal Powell stepped through her open door and said, "You wanted to leave early today so you could pick up the twins like normal. It's almost time for you to check outta here." He paused for but a moment and added, "I'm stopping by right now because I'm wondering how you're feeling about your first day."

Ever since she'd sent Principal Powell the email accepting his job offer, Shawntriece had been second guessing her decision. While talking to Principal Powell earlier in the day, she'd inadvertently let him in on her reservations, even going as far as telling the man she hadn't shared with her daughters the possibility of her working at their school. During their conversation, she'd expressed the desire to keep everything as normal as possible for her daughters for today. It had been Principal Powell who suggested she leave early and pick up Bria and Sierra like usual, breaking her news once they arrived home. Shawntriece was grateful for his suggestion and thought it was a great idea.

She smiled. "My first day here was great. As I was telling you this morning, I had my doubts." She shook her head and added, "But not anymore. I think this job is gonna turn out to be exactly what I need. The staff here is so friendly —," her smile faltered, "— and nobody's cutthroat like at my old job. Don't get me wrong," she hastily added, "overall, I enjoyed being an executive."

Principal Powell nodded in understanding. "I'm glad you see this opportunity as a blessing, Ms. Avery. God shows up and shows out when we least expect it. I'm certainly happy to have you on board." He smiled. "I hate to admit it, but I hate conducting interviews." A laugh. "I gotta tell ya'…you saved a brotha a whole lotta trouble."

She smiled again. "Yep, a blessing."

As soon as those words slipped past Shawntriece's lips, she couldn't help but think to herself: *A blessing? Why in the world would I say something like that?*

Noticing the slightly troubled look that had suddenly appeared on his new employee's face, Principal Powell asked, "Is everything alright, Miss Avery?"

Interested in making a quick save, Shawntriece placed a smile on her face and said, "Yes, everything's fine."

Principal Powell grinned again and gave his Smartwatch a meaningful little glance. "Good…I guess you'd better get out of here then. You don't wanna be late picking up Bria and Sierra. The end-of-day bell's gonna be ringing in about four minutes."

* * *

Later that Evening:

Shawntriece tucked the twins into their matching beds and made her way out of their bedroom. Her girls were actually going to sleep a full twenty minutes later than their normal bedtime. After they'd had dinner that evening, Shawntriece had told them about her new job at their school. Bria and Sierra's excitement had been in overdrive ever since. Shawntriece had thought for a moment that she was never gonna get them settled in for the night.

Smiling as she made her way to the kitchen to fix herself a relaxing cup of lavender tea, Shawntriece couldn't help but think to herself: *At least they're happy about me working at Higher Ground.*

She knew beyond a shadow of a doubt that some kids wouldn't exactly be pleased to have their parent working at their school.

She was on her second cup of tea when her cell phone began ringing.

"Well, how was your first day, Shawny? You *are* accepting the job, aren't you? You didn't go down there to that school and turn that man's generous offer down, did you?"

Shawntriece let out a short, dry laugh, tinged with a slight hint of irony. "Alright… Which one of those questions you want me to answer first, RoShonda?"

Shawntriece could practically *hear* her sibling rolling her eyes through the phone connection when she said, "Shawntriece…did you take the job or not?"

"What I *should* do is leave you in suspense—," she laughed, "—but I'm sure one of the girls are gonna drop the ball when you take them over to mama's place for baking day tomorrow afternoon."

"You took it! Thank God," RoShonda exclaimed.

"Yeah, I took the job, Shonda. You can stop worrying now."

"I just want what's best for my sissy. Plus," she laughed, "maybe now that you're gonna have a paycheck rolling in again, we can get back to having fun little outings like we used to."

It was Shawntriece's turn to shake her head and roll her eyes. "You know goodness well that the reason we haven't been going out as often is Brayden." Grinning, she hmphed. "He's who you've been spending all your free time with."

RoShonda couldn't stop herself from slowly lifting the corners of her lips in a smile. "Alright, hon… You got me on that one. But I'm still happy for you, Shawntriece. I think this job is gonna be good for you."

Shawntriece couldn't help but agree. So much so that she was looking forward to her second day.

CHAPTER NUMBER SEVEN

Shawntriece was the type of person who believed in giving her job her all. That's why she and the girls arrived at Higher Ground Academy at 7:05 a.m. the following morning — a full twenty-five minutes before the school was supposed to officially open for the day.

Rubbing her eyes, Bria looked out the window then frowned at her mother from the backseat of the car. "We're the only ones here, mama."

"Yeah, mama," Sierra seconded.

Shawntriece grimaced. She was sure that Principal Powell had told her that he usually arrived at the school by 7 o'clock. *I guess he's running a little late*, she reasoned to herself.

Just as she thought that, she heard a car pulling into the spot beside hers — the spot that had a sign on the pavement that read: *Reserved for the Principal*.

"Never mind, mama," Sierra shouted in an excited voice. "It's Shanequa and her dad!"

The twins grabbed their backpacks and scrambled out the car. As Shawntriece witnessed Shanequa doing the same, she picked up her briefcase and she, too, stepped out into the cool, autumn air.

"Good morning, Ms. Avery," Shanequa said, flashing a toothy smile.

Shawntriece smiled right back. "Good morning, Shanequa. It looks like you're ready to have a really good day at school today."

"Yes, ma'am."

"Good morning, ladies," Principal Powell greeted, grinning as well.

"Good morning, Mr. Powell," the twins said in unison.

Shawntriece looked her boss in the eye and flashed another smile. "Good morning, sir."

He shook his head and gave her a mock accusatory look. Then he chuckled. "Remember from yesterday…it's *Mr. Powell*. Principal Powell…sir…all of that is a little too formal for me. I try to avoid titles like that as much as I can."

"Right," she said. "Sorry, Mr. Powell."

He flashed another grin. "Much better. Thank you. Now that we got that out the way, let me unlock the building so we can get this show on the road. Neek normally waits in my office until her homeroom teacher clocks in for the day. Bria and Sierra are welcome to wait in your office—," he eyed the twins and chuckled, "—but I suspect they're gonna want to wait in my office with Shanequa."

"Yes! We wanna wait with Shanequa, momma."

Shanequa nodded her head in agreement. "Can they, Ms. Avery?"

Shawntriece laughed. "Sure, I don't see why not."

Principal Powell deactivated the electronic lock and held the front door open for all four of the females. "After you, ladies."

* * *

The day consisted of Shawntriece really digging into her administrative duties for the school. She hadn't expected that being a principal would be an easy job, but it looked like it was going to be a little more challenging than what she'd anticipated. Principal Powell had introduced her to the student body by taking her to each classroom and making a semiformal type of introduction. That segment of her day had been the easy part. It was all the legalities and red tape that she was having to familiarize herself with that was going to be the challenge.

An hour before school was slated to let out, Principal Powell knocked on Shawntriece's open door and stepped into her office space. "I see you're hard at work comparing last autumn's and this autumn's test scores for Ms. Carter's homeroom. I'm glad to see you're really digging in and taking your new job by the horns."

"Yeah. I'm really digging in alright… It's a lot to dig into."

"It'll get better as you become more familiar with the job. You're more than capable of handling this position. I could tell that this morning when you gave me that recommendation on Ms. Carter's classroom set up. Your recommendation is gonna save the school close to a grand." He smiled. "The school board and I like cutting our costs because it allows us to do more for our students."

"Right."

Shawntriece had to admit that getting Principal Powell's approval and praise felt good. She took her attention away from the papers she'd been working on, reached into her desk and pulled out a manila folder. "Speaking of saving money, I see that we have a contract with Turner Landscaping—," her eyes met his, "— they're charging us too much. We need to call around and get some comparison quotes. Then we can negotiate with Turner for a cheaper price. I'm sure they probably don't wanna lose our business over five hundred dollars or so per month. That's how much I estimate we'll save." She smiled. "I did a little bit of research online myself this morning."

"Wow… Impressive. I'mma have to see if I can give you overtime," he kidded.

"Overtime…I'm open to that. But just not today. I have to make sure the twins make it to their baking class this afternoon."

He nodded in acknowledgement of her statement. "Oh yeah… Neek told me about that." He chuckled. "In fact, she won't *stop* telling's me about it. We were talking about it this morning on the way to school…I'm sure we'll be talking about it again when it's time to go home."

Shawntriece laughed. "You should take her to today's class session. Or if you're too busy, she can go with me and my girls. The class is actually being offered and taught by my mother. My mom owns a bakery in the Renaissance Center in the northeast part of town. She gives baking classes once per week on Tuesdays. The 2nd and 4th Tuesdays of the month are dedicated to the kids."

She smiled. "Parents are encouraged to join in, of course."

A contemplative expression showed up on Principal Powell's face. "I love spoiling and surprising my little girl from time to time. This is last minute notice… Do I have to RSVP? Do you think your mom has room for two more?"

"No reservation's necessary." Shawntriece moved her eyelid in a conspiratorial little wink. "And if there was one, I'm sure my mom would bend the rules a little bit to accommodate my wonderful new boss, who just happens to be the dad of my twins' new best friend."

He chuckled. "It's a go then."

"Yep." She pulled her cell phone out her purse. "Let me text you the address. FYI, it starts at four."

* * *

Minutes after Principal Powell left her office, Shawntriece realized that she needed some paperclips to separate a report she'd been thumbing through and analyzing. Since she didn't have any on hand, she decided to make her way to the front office to ask the school's secretary for a couple.

Cassandra Byrd, the secretary, looked up from her computer monitor as soon as she heard Shawntriece come into her space. The middle-aged woman, skin the color of butterscotch, smiled and said, "I heard you talking to Mr. Powell when I walked past your office door a few minutes ago. I guess women nowadays don't waste no time letting a man know their interested in them. Back in my day, a young lady never woulda asked a man out. The man was supposed to do all that." She tsked. "You part of that women's lib movement, ain't chu?"

In Shawntriece's eyes, almost everything that Ms. Byrd had just said was inappropriate. However, at the same time, it was all so preposterous that Shawntriece couldn't help but laugh and say, "Me, asking Mr. Powell out? That's definitely not what happened. I haven't been working here long, but my girls have been students here for a minute, so, I've seen the way half the single, female parents 'round here seem to fall all over him…trying to get his attention and whatnot—," she hmphed. "—but you can trust and believe that I'm *not* one of them. I actually have better things to do with my time. A woman can't get anywhere in life if she's busy running after some man. I was inviting Mr. Powell's daughter on an outing with my twins…that's what you heard going on, Ms. Byrd. Mr. Powell's baby and my girls are gonna take a baking class together this afternoon."

Ms. Byrd had been working for Principal Powell for six years. In her eyes, she'd taken him under her wing somewhere during that time span. So, she felt like she'd been acting in the single father's best interest when she'd just approached Shawntriece about being on the make for him.

However, realizing that the gorgeous, young lady standing in front of her frowning was dead serious about what she'd just said, Ms. Byrd couldn't help but think to herself: *I ain't gotta worry about her coming up in here causing no trouble for Calvary.*

Shawntriece knew her answer before she even asked her next question. But since she wanted to lighten the mood in the room, she decided to tease Ms. Byrd by slyly asking, "You not trying to warn me off of him cause you want a piece of Mr. Powell for yourself, are you, Ms. Byrd?"

The heat of a blush rose up in Ms. Byrd's cheeks as she said, "Chile, please. I know black don't crack, but I'm almost sixty years old. I'm old enough to be Calvary's… um, I mean Mr. Powell's mama." She paused for but a moment then added, "I know all the female employees at this school are called *Miss This or Miss That*, but I'm a missus…as in M-R-S with a period. Mrs. You heard me? I actually have a husband who I love very much, thank you."

The look on Mrs. Byrd's face was comical to Shawntriece, so much so that she had to suppress her grin. "Ok," Shawntriece simply said. "Moving on to what I came up here for…I was hoping you have a couple of paperclips I can use."

Deciding that she liked their newest employee, Mrs. Byrd smiled as she reached into her desk and said, "Sure do, babydoll. Here you go. Hope y'all enjoy the little class you're going to."

* * *

Bria grabbed Shanequa's right hand, Sierra grabbed her left, and the three girls took off running towards the back of the room where the baking class was being conducted.

"Grandma! Grandma! This is our bestest friend in the whoooole wide world. Her name's Shanequa!"

Left standing with Principal Powell in the entry door to the work area, Shawntriece grinned and said, "I knew that was gonna happen the second we got here. My girls can't stop talking about their best friend, Shanequa… It's Shanequa this and Shanequa that. I swear I hear your daughter's name so much in my house that sometimes I look over my shoulder 'cause I think she's living with us," she kidded.

Principal Powell gave Shawntriece a smile in return. "Ditto. The names *Bria* and *Sierra* are bouncing off the walls in my house." His smile disappeared when he added, "I feel blessed that my daughter has two good friends in her life, though."

Something in the way he said what he'd just said let Shawntriece know there was something more to his statement. There was a vulnerability in his eyes that she hadn't been expecting to see there. Shawntriece had a big heart. So, despite only knowing her boss on a surface type of level, it made her want to ask him what was wrong and if she could do anything to help him.

However, they were in the company of twenty or so other people, which made the type of conversation she suspected they needed to have somewhat impossible. Plus, the look disappeared from his eyes almost as quickly as it had arrived.

Principal Powell looked around the room, taking in the six circular tables that were arranged in two lines of three. "Should we go ahead and claim a table for ourselves and the girls?" he asked.

Shawntriece laughed and pointed towards the front. "Actually, Bria and Sierra always sit at that table right there when they come to baking class."

As if on cue, the twins each grabbed one of Shanequa's hands and skipped with her to the table Shawntriece had just pointed to.

With the twinkle back in his eye again, Principal Powell chuckled. "I see that you're right, Ms. Avery."

* * *

The baking class was an overwhelming success, so much so that Principal Powell signed himself and Shanequa up for the upcoming session. Shanequa was so excited about the prospect that she was still talking about the class as her dad tucked her into bed.

"I really, really, really had a good time, daddy."

Principal Powell handed his daughter her teddy bear, Mrs. Snuggles, and asked, "You did?"

She nodded her little head. "Yep. I did. It was so much fun. Me, you, Bria, Sierra, Ms. Avery…all working together. I can't wait 'til next week when we *all* do it again!"

Principal Powell couldn't help but smile — for lots of reasons, one beyond the obvious. His baby girl had only been two years old — almost three — when her mother had died. It had been almost four years ago — and Shanequa had been really young — but Principal Powell knew that his daughter had never really gotten over losing her mom. Shanequa, once a bubbly, talkative child, had withdrawn into a shell and had barely talked to anyone after that time. That's why Principal Powell had been ecstatic when he'd noticed her making friends with the twins. And it was also why he'd been so happy to see her having a good time today at the baking class.

He bent down and placed a soft kiss on his child's forehead. "I'm glad you enjoyed yourself, Neek-Bear… And I can't wait until we go again, too. Now, lights out or you won't be able to roll outta bed tomorrow for school."

CHAPTER NUMBER EIGHT

At exactly 11:56, Shawntriece stood up from her desk at Higher Ground Academy and made her way to the school's boardroom for her noon meeting with Principal Powell.

When he heard the boardroom door opening, Calvary looked up from the papers he was pouring over. His eyes met Shawntriece's and he said, "I know I told you we'd be working on revising the 3rd grade math curriculum, but I got an email from the schoolboard… They want a revision on the 5th grade curriculum first."

Shawntriece smiled. "Lucky for me that I've been brushing up on third through fifth grade math concepts and standards this week. I believe I can handle it."

He tented his fingers in front of himself and studied her for a few seconds, prompting Shawntriece to tilt her eyebrow and ask, "Is there something wrong, Principal Powell?"

He shook his head. "No. I was just reflecting on how your drive and determination makes you a perfect fit for this job. I'm glad the Lord led you my way. What you lack in experience, you make up for in ambition and commitment." He smiled. "My baby girl is happy to have you here, too. She can't wait until we meet you and the twins for another baking class."

Shawntriece felt the heat of a blush rising in her cheeks from his compliment. She'd been complimented by her bosses at previous places of employment;

however, Calvary Powell's praise was sincere. Heartfelt even. Shawntriece felt it right down in her bones.

"Thanks for your kind words, Principal Powell — they certainly are appreciated. And as for the baking class, I'm looking forward to it, too. Your Shanequa is a sweetheart, and those little jokes — the ones you seem to like to make *all* the time — crack me up. Yesterday was fun."

"Yes, it was fun. Shanequa and I *both* enjoyed it."

Shawntriece grinned. "But I'm sure you and I both know that it doesn't take much to make six-year-olds happy…especially outgoing kids like our girls… Kids who are extroverts."

Shawntriece had been expecting Principal Powell to give a quick reply of agreement to her last comment. She wasn't expecting to see the shadow that passed across his face. "Yeah," he slowly said. "That's the case with *most* six-year-olds, but my Shanequa hasn't always been so —how would I say it? Bubbly… And especially not with people who aren't family."

"You're kidding," she said in surprise. "The Shanequa who was making thumbprint cookies with us yesterday had an outgoing energy that's as bright as the sun sitting up there in the sky."

"Nope, I'm not kidding." He slowly curled his lips up in a smile. "What you witnessed is what I call in my mind the '*Twins Effect*'."

"Twins effect?"

"Yep." Seeing the look of confusion on her face he laughed and added, "More specifically, the Bria and Sierra effect. You see, Ms. Avery, my baby started pre-K here two years ago. But she was a lonely little thing who shied away from people and making friends. Her mother — my wife — passed away when she was two. Shanequa withdrew within herself when she figured out that her mother wouldn't be coming back to us." He grimaced. "I used to consider myself lucky if I heard my daughter say twenty words in a single day."

Shawntriece could see the pain in his eyes as he spoke of the tragedy. "I'm sorry to hear about your loss, Mr. Powell. And I'm sorry for how it affected that sweet little girl of yours."

"Thanks for your heartfelt sympathy, Ms. Avery. It makes me feel good right in here—," he patted his chest with his fist a few times, "—to know that someone cares."

He paused for a few seconds and said, "I admit that my daughter's still shy—," he finally smiled again, "—but her extreme shyness disappeared somewhat this year when she was placed in Ms. Donovan's first grade class with Bria and Sierra. Your daughters made sure that they always talked to and interacted with my Shanequa…you know, they insisted that she be a part of whatever was going on in their classroom. Their persistence finally drew my daughter out her shell. When she's around the twins, she's a little chatterbox. And she's talking more at home and other places, too."

He looked Shawntriece in the eye and chuckled. "I think I know where Bria and Sierra get their determination and persistence from." He winked. "And it's a good thing."

"Thank you for the compliment. I'm glad my girls are bringing about something positive." She smiled.

"Like I said, I can hardly believe that Shanequa's not an outgoing type of person. Either way, she's a sweetheart." Thinking about how the child had offered her assistance to anyone in their little group of who seemed like they needed help during their baking class, Shawntriece added, "She's so kind, polite, and helpful."

Like any proud parent who liked hearing good things about their kid, Principal Powell was positively beaming by this time. "Thank you," he said.

"No problem, it's the truth."

Shawntriece suddenly had an idea. "I normally take Bria and Sierra on an outing every Saturday. Since Shanequa's been having such a positive experience with my girls, I'd be happy if she tagged along with us. You could come with us if you like…I'm sure your presence would provide some balance for her that she'll probably appreciate. The twins and I are heading to the natural science center this weekend."

Using his thumb and forefinger, he pinched his chin in contemplation and said, "You know, I've actually been thinking about taking Neek there — it *is* right here in town — but I somehow hadn't gotten around to doing it." He grinned. "I think I'll take you up on your offer."

She smiled, too. "Good. I had planned on being there at eleven. Will eleven work for you?"

"Yep. Eleven will be perfect. Neek and I will meet you there in the parking lot. And on that note, you ready to get started on our project of the day?"

"Ready."

* * *

Later that Evening:

For as long as Shawntriece could remember, her sister, RoShonda, had been her go-to person whenever she took the twins out on the town and craved a little adult company. They were supposed to be going to the natural science center together on Saturday. Shawntriece had their upcoming visit on her mind as she walked out her twins' bedroom, done with tucking them in for the evening.

She pulled out her cell phone. Sitting on her overstuffed, tribal-style designer sofa, her thumbs began to fly as she composed a text message to her sister. She typed: *Two more are going with us to the natural science center on Saturday.*

Within a minute of pressing send, Shawntriece's cell phone was ringing.

"Okay, girl, who coming with us on Saturday? Don't tell me Vivian want us to take her bad tail kids. She's our cousin and all, but ain't no way—in nowhere—that I'm 'bout to be down for dealing with all that. Andre and Madison are a handful. I didn't know a seven-year-old and six-year-old could get into so much trouble. Instead of the terrible twos, those two are the terrible six and terrible seven. Mama told me this morning that Sister Clarice said that Andre and Madison were outside of the church pulling up weeds last Sunday. Then they came inside and tried to sell their little harvest to Pastor Heaton… Told him not to worry cause it was medicinal weed so it was legal."

Shawntriece laughed. "No, it's not Andre and Madison. I invited Principal Powell and his little girl, Shanequa…Bria and Sierra's best friend."

"Oh, that's a relief. Shanequa's well-behaved and unlike Andre and Madison, I don't see her getting us kicked out the science center." She paused for a second and said, "Wait a minute. You said Principal Powell's tagging along, right?"

"Yep."

"In that case, you won't need me to go, too. Brayden had wanted me to go with him to an architectural design show that they're having in Raleigh on Saturday. I told him I couldn't go because I had already made a prior commitment to you and the twins."

"We love your company, honey, but Bria, Sierra, and I will definitely be fine without you at the center. You should've told me about Brayden's event — I would've told you to go. Y'all have a good time—," she laughed, "—and post some pictures on Facebook so I can be nosy and see what all the fuss was about."

"I will, sis."

They talked for only a few minutes more. Then they disconnected their call and Shawntriece decided to surf the web a little before it was time for her to review the curriculum that she and Principal Powell had worked on earlier in the day.

She fired up her laptop and began checking her social media feed. She looked at the bottom of the screen at the list of people that the social media platform suggested she may know. She was surprised to see that "Calvary Powell" was included in the suggestion loop.

Shawntriece moved her computer's cursor and hovered over Calvary Powell's name, debating on whether or not she should click it. *Girl, now you up in here being nosy and acting like RoShonda*, she thought to herself. *Nope, you're just curious*, her brain countered. *A little curiosity never hurt nobody*.

Her inquisitive side won the battle and she clicked on the link. Unfortunately, when she landed on her boss' profile page, his account had been set to private, meaning that only social media friends of his could see his content.

Slightly embarrassed, Shawntriece shook her head. "Serves me right…that's what I get for being nosy," she muttered under her breath as she navigated back to her own social media page and went back to checking on updates from her online friends.

* * *

Across Town:

With his daughter already tucked into bed, Principal Powell grabbed his iPad and decided to do a little web surfing for enjoyment purposes. Sitting in his living room, he started with checking out the news and sports headlines. Somehow, he ended up on Facebook. As he checked out the social media feeds of his friends and family, he happened to catch a glance of the "People You May Know" banner at the bottom of his Facebook page. He was surprised to see Shawntriece Avery's smiling face amongst his friend recommendations. Her grin was infectious; it made him grin right along with her.

I wonder what type of things she likes to put on the Book, he mused to himself as he clicked on her link to find out.

Seeing that Shawntriece's profile was set to private, he didn't get very far in his endeavors.

Just send her a friend request.

"Nah, I shouldn't do that," he whispered under his breath. Why? Because he only allowed his family and personal friends to be a part of his online social media community. Part of his world.

But her kids are my daughter's best friends, he reasoned to himself. *The two of us — with Neek and the twins — have already been to two events together. And we're going on a third outing this weekend…not to mention the next baking class that's coming up week after next.*

He convinced himself to send the friend request. He smiled as he pressed the icon on his Facebook page.

* * *

Over at Shawntriece's House:

Shawntriece stifled a yawn and moved her hand to close her laptop. Just before she could accomplish her goal, her computer chimed, letting her know that she'd received another notification.

She reopened the laptop and checked her message: *Calvary Powell Sent You A Friend Request.*

What? She was surprised to see that. However, she smiled and clicked on the button to accept his offer of friendship. As she strolled through his online world, checking out photos he'd posted and whatnot, she thought to herself: *This isn't weird at all. His daughter is my girls' best friend. A smart parent would wanna know what the man's all about.*

She decided that she wanted to check out his family connections on Facebook, but before she could navigate to that portion of the website, her doorbell began ringing.

Shawntriece frowned; she wasn't expecting company. However, when the doorbell was followed by a door knock to the tune of the old song, *Somebody's Knocking at Your Door*, she realized that the unexpected visitor was RoShonda — RoShonda was the only one who knocked like that.

"Hey, boo," RoShonda said as she stepped in handing Shawntriece a Tupperware container. "I messed around and cooked a lasagna today anyway. Here you go, my babies can have them some for lunch tomorrow at school. I know how much Bria and Sierra love Auntie's special lasagna."

Shawntriece laughed. "Correct me if I'm wrong, but you're the one who said they didn't have you wrapped around their little fingers, right?"

Being the proud, doting aunt that she was, RoShonda laughed, too. "Busted." She pointed at the coffee table. "Same ol' Shawny…I see you're still bringing work home." She hmphed. "Girl, I love my job, but I ain't doing all of that. My free time is *my* free time."

"It's not *work*, little Miss Know-It-All," she teased. "I was actually on Facebook. Mr. Powell sent me a friend request and I accepted it. I was going through his profile and feed."

"You did what?"

"I was poking around on Facebook."

RoShonda shook her head. "No, not that part… The '*friend request*' part."

"Principal Powell sent me a friend request on Facebook and I accepted it." Shawntriece shrugged her shoulders. "It's no big deal, Shonda."

RoShonda cocked an eyebrow, indicating that she really didn't believe the words that had just casually fallen from her sibling's mouth. "No big deal, sweetie? What happened to, and I quote: *I keep a wide line between my personal life and my job*." She paused and added, "You're famous for saying that… You started saying it as soon as you graduated from college and got your first professional position over at Shugartsen."

"I wasn't looking at Calvary Powell as my boss when I accepted his friend request a half hour ago, Shonda. I was looking at him as the parent of Bria and Sierra's best friend... There's a big difference."

Shonda thought it was something more to her sister becoming Facebook friends with Calvary Powell, but she didn't feel like having that particular conversation with Shawntriece right now — it was approaching 8 o'clock and Shonda had to be at work by five in the morning. She smiled to herself. *I think my sissy is attracted to the man. But since she doesn't believe in relationships and dating, she's not gonna admit to having those types of feelings...at least not without a verbal fight.*

"Oh, okay," Shonda said, keeping her innermost thoughts to herself. "I put enough lasagna in there for you, too. I'mma head back home…I'm looking at an early morning."

"Alright, sis. Thanks for the lasagna."

As soon as she pulled out of Shawntriece's driveway, RoShonda told her car: *Call Angelica.*

"What's up, Shonda?" her big sister said in lieu of hello.

"Girl, you ain't even gonna believe this. I'm pulling off from Shawny's house, and right before I got there, she had accepted a Facebook request from her new boss, Principal Powell."

"What?" Angelica asked in disbelief.

"Yep. Our dear sister broke her own rule and let her boss become one of her friends on the Book. And she's letting him tag along with her to the Natural Science Center this Saturday… I was supposed to go with her, but she practically kicked my butt to the curb." She laughed. "Well, I gotta take that back, she invited him and his daughter to go with us. Then she told me I didn't have to go because she has him as her adult companion on the little trek." She added, "Sista girl is justifying all this by saying that Principal Powell's daughter is Bria and Sierra's best friend. What do you think about everything I just said?"

Contemplating the situation, Angelica was quiet for several seconds, prompting RoShonda to say, "Well…what do you think, honey?"

"On the surface it seems like Shawny has an attraction to the man. But you know her, she's not interested in a relationship. She's not giving no man her time of day." She frowned. "After what she went through, I can't say that I blame her. Having her innocence stolen, being raped at only fifteen years old changed our sister…and as you know, it wasn't for the better. Her psychological hurt is so deep that she couldn't even bring herself to get pregnant the natural way… She had to go get a sperm donor and be artificially inseminated. So, I wouldn't go getting my hopes up high if I were you, Shonda. There's probably nothing at all going on between Shawny and her boss."

"Yeah, you're probably right," RoShonda regrettably admitted. She felt like someone had just taken the wind out her sails. *Look at me and my wishful thinking. I gotta face what's probably the facts.*

CHAPTER NUMBER NINE

Shawntriece woke up from a deep, satisfying slumber on Saturday morning with a smile on her face. She was excited about the upcoming events of the day; she'd even just woken up from a dream about the Natural Science Center. Memories of the place were still in her mind, from a visit that she and the twins had made one time before when they were only two years old.

Principal Powell had told her yesterday at work that he, too, was really looking forward to the outing. Lying in bed, for some reason, Shawntriece began thinking about some of the pictures he'd posted on his Facebook page over the years…pictures she'd seen from poking around in his photo album section.

"He looked so happy with his wife in those pictures, and they had such a beautiful family. Him, his wife, Yvette, and their cute little baby girl," she whispered under her breath.

She began thinking about all the pictures he'd also posted of himself at various church events — one even from last week.

Your God allowed your beautiful wife to die in a traffic accident — no fault of yours or hers. How could you still believe that he's so merciful and loving? How could you still believe in him at all? Your daughter's still suffering the psychological damage from the tragedy. How can you still smile and profess allegiance to your quote-unquote precious Lord and Savior? She sucked her teeth. *Savior, indeed. Where did that get your wife? He certainly didn't save her.*

Just thinking about it all caused Shawntriece to shake her head.

Then hearing her girls begin to chatter in their bedroom, she knew it was time to get started with their day.

A couple of hours later, she and Principal Powell, ironically, rolled up in the parking lot at the Natural Science Center at the same time — ten minutes shy of their agreed upon meeting time.

"Morning ladies," Principal Powell said, as he and Shanequa exited their vehicles.

They all exchanged greetings, then they made their way into the large, sprawling building. After partaking of all the attractions that the center had to offer, Principal Powell said, "Wow, what an experience… I had fun, what about you guys?"

Of course, Shanequa and the twins agreed, loudly and excitedly, causing Shawntriece and Principal Powell, both, to laugh.

"In that case then, how about you guys let me treat you all to lunch." His eyes met Shawntriece's. "You and Bria and Sierra down for that?"

Not wanting their day to end, the twins each grabbed Shawntriece by the hand and begged, "Please, mama!"

Nodding her head and flashing a toothy grin, Shanequa joined the chorus.

Shawntriece laughed. "Alright, alright, you three. How could I turn such wonderful young ladies down."

"Thank you, mama!" the twins shouted.

"Thank you, Ms. Avery," Shanequa said, in a noticeably quieter, more subdued voice.

It was moments like this that Shawntriece believed what Principal Powell had been saying about his daughter normally being reclusive and non-verbal. Otherwise, Shantriece wouldn't have seen any signs that it was remotely possible that the cute-as-a-button little girl was a victim of behavioral issues — that the tragedy of losing her mother had afflicted her so.

Looking directly at the three youngsters, Principal Powell said, "Well, I think I recall somebody talking about how much they like Mexican food while we were looking at the reptile exhibit. How about Moe's?"

"Yes!" the girls shouted, Shanequa included.

Principal Powell looked up and shifted his eye gaze to Shawntriece. "That okay with you, mama?"

"Yep, I could use a burrito. Moe's will be just fine."

The group of five was making its way out the science center when they heard, "Calvary Powell is that you?"

Calvary smiled at the pretty sista with the cute bob haircut who'd just stopped them from exiting the facility. "It's me in the flesh," he said.

The newcomer looked down at Shanequa and smiled. "Hey, Neeky Poo. I guess you had yourself a real good time today."

Shawntriece couldn't help but notice that Shanequa didn't smile in return. Instead, reminiscent of a snail retreating into its shell, she did a shy little hand wave and moved closer to her father's leg, almost as if she was seeking shelter or protection from him.

The woman looked back up at Principal Powell. "You should've told me the two of y'all were coming up here today — you and Shanequa," she specified. "Me and Sean would've gotten here earlier. He's in the car with mama by the way. For some reason, he took his shoes off and she's putting them back on for him. I'm going ahead and buying our entry tickets."

The woman suddenly wagged a finger between Shawntriece and Principal Powell. "Wait a minute, y'all up here on a date or something?"

Principal Powell shook his head. "No. Our girls are best friends. We're just treating them to a day out on the town. We're on our way to lunch right now. Tasha, this is Shawntriece Avery—"

Tasha interrupted him with, "You don't have to introduce us, Calvary. We met at Shanequa's little birthday party a few weeks ago at Chuck E. Cheese's. Remember?"

Shawntriece turned her lips up in a friendly little smile. "It's nice to see you again, Tasha."

Grinning, Tasha said, "Likewise, likewise." Then she looked at Principal Powell. "I guess I'll let y'all get on your way, Calvary. See you in church tomorrow. Okay?"

"God willing, I'll be there," he said in response. "You know a brotha really be trying not to miss out on the Word."

Tasha let out a little giggle, one that sounded decidedly flirtatious to Shawntriece's ears. "Amen to that, Calvary. See you tomorrow."

Shawntriece had to fight the urge to roll her eyes in irritation as Tasha walked away with a slightly exaggerated switch to her hips. *She definitely has some type of crush on the good principal here. I hate it when women make moves like that…she's just making herself seem desperate.*

"Let's keep it moving, ladies. We don't want Moe's to give out of food before we get there." Principal Powell followed his comment with a chuckle, one which the three six-year-olds responded to with giggles of their own.

"You're funny, Mr. Powell," Bria said.

Sierra nodded in agreement to her sibling's statement and Shanequa — emerging from her shell again — said, "Yeah, daddy."

* * *

Later that Night:

"Well, since you didn't call me to tell me how you and my nieces' day went, I decided I would call you and ask how everything played out. And since I know you're gonna ask…me and Brayden's day was phenomenal. Girl, I think I'm gonna end up marrying that brotha. I just gotta wait for him to pop the question." She laughed. "Or I can take a page from Great Aunt Shelia's book and pull out my shotgun and force him to take me down the aisle."

Thinking of their dearly departed great aunt, Shawntriece couldn't help but smile. Then she said, "Where you gonna get a shotgun from, Shonda? Or better yet, how are you going to bring yourself to use it?

You know when me and Angelique tried to get you to take target practice classes with us, you were scared to even pick up the pistol. And it was a little bitty thing…a 9-millimeter."

"Whateva… You know I believe in non-violence."

"Me, too, honey. But I feel like a female should at least know how to use a weapon. You never know when that type of knowledge will come in handy. Of course, I don't keep a gun in the house, but when Bria and Sierra get old enough, I'm gonna make sure they take some classes. Isaiah Chapter 8 in your own Bible tells you to fear nothing but God. A little bitty handgun shouldn't have you running scared."

On rare occasions, Shawntriece would quote scripture. Those instances always gave RoShonda hope that her older sibling would come back to the winning side.

RoShonda normally would've told Shawntriece something like: *There you go, I heard you quoting the good book…look atcha.* She decided against it this time. She didn't want anything to jeopardize hearing how her sister's day had gone with Calvary Powell.

"Alright, Shawny…I hear you, boo. Now tell me how your day with Principal Powell played out. I'm sure the twins enjoyed themselves."

Shawntriece proceeded to give her sister a play-by-play of her day. When she got to the part that involved Tasha Parker, she shook her head and said, "I couldn't help but feel bad for her, honey…she was doing the most. You hear me? It seemed like she was trying to practically throw herself on the man. If her son hadn't been with her on her little visit to the science center, I suspect she would've invited herself to lunch with me, Mr. Powell, and the girls. And then when she finally walked away to find her son, she was switching so hard and not paying attention that her right hip knocked into a stuffed animal display. Homegirl brought the whole shelf down. Chile, there was lions, tigers, and bears everywhere." She shook her head. "Just pathetic, Shonda."

To Shonda, it sounded like her sibling was irritated because Tasha was trying to pick up the man she'd gone out with for the day. Shonda felt like Shawntriece's little attitude was proof that she kinda-sorta liked Principal Powell. Instead of saying anything about it, Shonda laughed in response to hearing about Tasha Parker's antics.

Giggling, RoShonda said, "Well, hopefully y'all won't run into Tasha when you and Principal Powell take the girls to the African Art class next weekend."

"You're not going with us?" Shawntriece asked in surprise.

RoShonda laughed again. "Nope. Me and Brayden are heading to the coast. Yeah, it's autumn, but it's still pretty out there this time of year. His grandparents live in Myrtle Beach and they had said they wanted to meet me. We're staying with his grands for the weekend — separate bedrooms, of course… A'int gon' be no shacking up and devil making for me. I'll be back Sunday night."

"His grandparents wanna meet you? Wow, I guess you guys *are* getting serious. Interesting."

"What? No congratulations?"

Shawntriece loved her sister and wanted to see her happy. So, instead of saying anything that would ruin the moment, she said, "You know how I feel about relationships, honey. But if Brayden's making you happy, congratulations."

"Thank you, Shawny." RoShonda smiled. "I know you had to dig deep to say all that. I love you, girl."

"And I love you, too, bighead."

RoShonda laughed at the pet name from childhood, then playfully added, "I'mma tell mama you called me a name."

"Blabbermouth," Shawntriece kidded.

"Okay, okay, Shawny… You was always one to take it to the next level. Goodnight."

* * *

Across Town:

Principal Powell stepped out of the shower and shrugged into his bathrobe. It had been a long, but enjoyable day. He was grateful for it.

Minutes later, he said his prayers for the night and pulled out his cellphone. He grinned as he began swiping through the photos they'd taken at the science center. Himself, Shanequa, Bria, Sierra, and Ms. Avery.

Ms. Avery. He stopped on a photo that he'd captured of her play-posing in front of the aquatics tank, pretending to be a fish. *She has a great smile*, he thought to himself. *And kind eyes. I can see why my brother said she's a cutie. She's pretty. Very attractive.*

Realizing exactly where his train of thought was taking him, he frowned. This was the first time since losing his wife that he'd stopped and reflected on another woman's prettiness.

He abruptly placed his cell phone on his nightstand and picked up the framed photo of his wife, Yvette, that he kept by his bedside. He lovingly traced the outline of her beautiful face. "You had a great smile and kind eyes, too, sweetheart. I miss you, babe."

Normally when Principal Powell uttered words like that about the woman he had promised forever, he'd feel a deep pain in his chest — really in his very soul. He was surprised to realize that at that moment, he wasn't feeling the ache, the pain. All he was experiencing was happiness as he reminisced on the love that he and Yvette had had for each other, the good times they'd shared.

He placed the picture back in its rightful place. He was certain that he'd always love Mrs. Yvette Powell. "And that's on life," he whispered under his breath as he turned off the nightstand light, shortly thereafter, drifting off to sleep.

CHAPTER NUMBER TEN

"Mr. Powell, good morning. I'm about to make myself a cup of coffee…you want one, too?" Shawntriece turned her lips up in a smile in greeting. "Two creams and one lump of sugar, right?"

Principal Powell looked up from his office desk and shook his head. "No thank you, Ms. Avery."

The man had smiled at her when he'd made his comment, but the smile didn't seem very warm. It didn't really reach his eyes. *It's like he's trying to be reserved or something*, Shawntriece thought to herself. *Like he's trying to hold back.*

"Is there anything wrong?" she asked in concern.

"No. Everything's fine, Ms. Avery. Thank you."

Shawntriece could read people pretty well most of the time. She knew when she was being dismissed. "Okay," she finally said. "I'll be on my way then. After I'm done with the budget report, I'll head over and relieve the substitute teacher in Ms. Johnson's class…she just paged me and said she's feeling nauseous."

Principal Powell had told himself that when he made it to school on Monday morning, he was going to be more restrained with Shawntriece — intentionally. The fact that he'd been dreaming about her the past couple of nights — ever since they'd taken the girls on the outing to the science center — was prompting this particular response from him. The dreams had been strictly PG, but the fact that he'd dreamed about his new employee at all was bothering him.

However, the slight tinge of worry that he heard in her voice when she said she'd be taking over Ms. Johnson's class for the day took him from his place of reserve. He wanted to ease her concerns.

He couldn't help but slowly raise his lips in a warm, genuine smile and say, "Teaching is like riding a bicycle, Shawntriece. Once you learn how, you never forget. Once you get in that classroom with those kids in a few, it's gonna feel just like old times. I used to feel the same way when I first became an administrator, as opposed to being a classroom instructor. Most principals are the backup when a suitable substitute can't be found. Every time I had to substitute teach, I felt a mini panic attack coming on."

Shawntriece had felt like she'd been doing a good job at hiding the fact that she was scared out her wits of going into that classroom in less than an hour.

He softly chuckled a couple of times. "Don't worry, you still have a pretty good poker face. It's just that I've started to pick up on certain nuances about you. In other words, I'm starting to be able to tell when something's worrying you. Hint, hint…your nose tilts up a little bit to the left," he jokingly conspired.

"For real? You're kidding. I had *no* idea I did that."

He nodded his head. "Yep, you do. I noticed it when we were at the science center the other day. Whenever one of the girls got out of your sight, you'd do it…right before you started looking around for them."

"Hm, interesting."

He grinned. "Yes, it is. And like I said, you're gonna be okay in that classroom. It really is just like riding a bike."

"In that case then, thanks for your advice. Lord knows the positive affirmation speech that I was giving myself in my head wasn't working." She laughed.

"You're welcome, Ms. Avery."

Seconds after Shawntriece walked away, heading towards the canteen area of their common office space, a little voice in Principal Powell's head said: *How did being cool and reserved work out for ya, bruh? You totally bombed it. Next thing you know, you're gonna wanna be in there literally holding her hand while she teaches the class.*

Principal Powell felt like mentally telling his subconscious to shut up. However, he opted to mumble under his breath, instead, saying, "I can't be holding a back-and-forth conversation with myself in my head… Then I'mma know I'm cray, cray for real. Mama always said it's okay to talk to yourself as long as you don't answer back."

He frowned. He couldn't understand what it was about Shawntriece Avery that was causing him to act the way that he was acting recently. "Lord, please just let it pass."

* * *

Later that Afternoon:

"While you were teaching, I peeked in on you a couple of times when you weren't looking… You were great in there. I was right, wasn't I?"

Standing outside the school with Principal Powell handling student pickup duty, Shawntriece nodded her head. "Yes, you were right. I got caught up in teaching using the lesson plan that Ms. Johnson left, and somehow, it didn't even feel like I'd been out of the classroom for close to a decade." She laughed. "Are we having an '*I Told You So*' moment, Principal P?"

He didn't answer her question. Instead, he joked, "Principal P…that kinda makes me sound like a superhero. I think I like the sound of that." He smiled. "And yes, we're having an "*I Told You So*' moment…but in the good type of way."

She thought about all the off-the-clock time that the man standing beside her devoted to school duties, about how much he genuinely cared about the kids under his helm. *He's certainly a superhero in a lot of these kids' eyes.*

"I don't think you have to worry about not being a superhero, Mr. Powell. I think a lot of our student's already think you're a hero of sorts."

Overhearing the adults' conversation, one of the fourth graders at the school laughed and held up his hand towards Principal Powell for a high-five. "Yeah, Principal P. Ms. Avery's right."

Principal Powell slapped hands with the ten-year-old then sternly, but playfully said, "In that case Hakeem, I guess I'm not gonna have to worry about any of your teachers sending you to my office for talking in class this week… Right?"

"Yes, sir, Mr. Super P!" Spotting his mother's car pulling up to the pickup spot, he added, "See you tomorrow, Mr. Super P…you too Ms. Avery!"

They both waved goodbye to the child, then Principal Powell turned to Shawntriece. "Mr. Super P…I think you might've just started something, Ms. Avery."

"Don't worry, Mr. Super P," she teased. "By the time you get back to school next Monday, he'll have forgotten all about it."

"That's right. You and I have the administrator's conference to attend on this Thursday and Friday. And Wednesday — day after tomorrow — is an official school holiday. I'll be out of sight and out of mind from Hakeem for five whole days."

"Yep." She laughed. "That'll work to your advantage. And on a different note, as for the administrator's conference, I'm very comfortable with participating in that. It's right up my alley."

He grinned. "Given your corporate background, I assumed that would be the case. I see no need for us to take two separate cars to Raleigh for the event. I'll be happy to drive both days if you'd like me to…an hour and a half on the interstate isn't too bad. Although I do admit that I hate Raleigh traffic."

"That sounds like a great idea," Shawntriece answered. She laughed. "I never give up the opportunity to be in the passenger seat for a change. Wait a minute, you're a safe driver, aren't you?" She began ticking off on her fingers, "No points, revocations, suspensions, DWIs—"

He interrupted her with a chuckle. "I'm a safe driver. I can get you a copy of my driving record from the DMV if you need it."

Shawntriece squinted one eye, pretending to analyze him. "Um, okay…I think I can trust you. You're practically a superhero after all."

He laughed. "Right."

* * *

It wasn't until he was at home that night, getting ready for bed, that Principal Powell began making a mental analysis of his day. He thought back to his and Shawntriece's conversation as they performed student-pick-up duty together. Before heading outside of the school for the end-of-day activity, Principal Powell had told himself that he was going to place his reserved behavior with Shawntriece Avery into full effect — he'd told himself that he wasn't going to drop the ball like he'd done earlier in the day. He now realized that his afternoon attempts to be cool and reserved with her had been a fail. The second he'd gotten outside with Shawntriece, he'd started laughing and kidding around with her like they were old friends. Of course, he'd kept a professional demeanor about himself, but still, he'd let loose and enjoyed the moment. All twenty-five minutes of it.

He let a breath out in a tired sounding sigh. "Why is Shawntriece Avery staying on my mind? Why do I keep thinking about her off and on throughout the day?" He shook his head. "I don't understand it, Lord. All I can do is have faith that you'll reveal all to me in due time."

He said his prayers and turned off the lamp on his nightstand. He was hoping that he didn't dream about Shawntriece again tonight.

CHAPTER NUMBER ELEVEN

"I knew since school was out for today that you'd be home this morning. Can I borrow some of your tools until the weekend, bro?"

School holidays were just about the only time that Principal Powell allowed himself the luxury of sleeping in. Seeing that it was only eight-thirty in the morning, he hadn't gotten in too much sleeping-in time today.

Principal Powell frowned at his younger brother. "You're going on thirty, Zay. It's about time for you to get your own toolset, don't you think?"

Xavier wasn't used to his sibling being grouchy, so, the response he'd just received surprised him. He walked into the front door that Principal Powell was holding open. "What's wrong with you, Cal? You wake up on the wrong side of the bed this morning or nah?"

Principal Powell blew out a breath and shook his head. "Get the toolbox, Zay. You know where it is. I'm about to make myself some coffee."

Heading towards the door that led to the garage, Xavier said, "Make enough for me, too. You buy that good Ethiopian stuff… I ain't about to miss out on that."

By the time Xavier made it back inside the main part of the house, Principal Powell was pouring himself his first cup of Joe.

"You didn't pour me a cup?" Xavier asked in a joking tone.

"Nope."

"Man, you *are* a grouch this morning." Xavier brought his eyebrows together in a grimace. "Seriously though, what's wrong, bruh?"

Do I tell my little brother that I'm irritated because I kept dreaming last night about a certain sista with a beautiful smile and even lovelier deep brown eyes?

"It's getting close to the anniversary of the accident," Xavier said, thinking he'd figured out what had gotten his normally cheerful sibling in such a bad mood. "It's in a few weeks." He patted Principal Powell on the back. "She was my sister-in-law. I loved her like blood. I miss her too, man."

Principal Powell was aware of the quickly approaching anniversary of the tragedy. He was ashamed to admit to Xavier that that wasn't the problem.

"The first year you were mourning something terrible and I thought you were gonna need some counseling. But then after that, with each year that passed, you seemed to get better. Seems like you're regressing, bruh. You wanna talk about it?"

His younger brother had just earned his master's degree in clinical psychology a year ago, so, even though it would feel a little weird, Principal Powell knew that Xavier was somewhat qualified to listen to his problems. Surprising even himself, he said, "It's crazy, but I keep having dreams about me and Shawntriece Avery going around town, um…doing things togeher…um…going places." *Bad idea*, he thought to himself, almost as soon as the words had come out his mouth.

"The new principal you hired?"

In for a penny, in for a pound. "Yep," he replied.

"Hmm, interesting. On the surface it would seem like you have yourself a little crush on the lovely Principal Avery. B-u-u-u-t, if one were to delve a little deeper, I'd say that having thoughts about Ms. Avery represents you completing the grieving process for Yvette. I hadn't said anything, but for the past couple of years, I've been thinking you're a victim of incomplete grief."

"What?"

Xavier nodded his head. "Incomplete grief," he repeated. "You see, bruh, you always told us that you'd love Yvette forever and that she was irreplaceable. However, to complete the grieving process, you have to mentally let Yvette go. When we lose someone we love, major changes —like officially letting go — often happen around the anniversary date of the tragic loss. So, stop worrying. You probably don't really have a thing for that hottie you just hired… You're just finally completing the healing process. I'm surprised it didn't happen sooner than this. Having thoughts about another female is just a byproduct of the process of completing your mourning." Deciding to step down from the role of professional, Xavier suddenly grinned and said, "Since I charge sixty dollars per hour, that'll be twelve bucks."

Principal Powell chuckled as he picked up the second coffee cup that he'd placed on the counter and poured dark, hot brew into it. "Here you go, Zay. Paid in full. Thanks."

As soon as Xavier walked out of his home, toolbox in tow, Principal Powell sat on his sofa with his laptop in front of him. He respected the master's degree in clinical psychology that his brother had earned, but he couldn't help but think to himself: *This is my kid brother that I'm getting advice from. He's only twenty-nine years old — barely a 'real' adult.*

Despite his doubts, a half hour later, various peer-approved research articles that Principal Powell found online in reference to incomplete grief gave credence to what his sibling had just been telling him.

"I can stop worrying about how much Shawntriece Avery's been on my mind. What a relief. Now I can actually look forward to the administrator's conference we're gonna be attending together tomorrow and Friday. I always enjoy those conferences…they're a welcome change of pace."

* * *

The Following Morning:

Principal Powell's mother had taught him to be a gentleman. Accordingly, he opened the door on the passenger's side of his SUV for his travel companion. When he caught a whiff of the perfume that Shawntriece was wearing, he wasn't even concerned that he immediately told himself: *That's a beautiful fragrance…just like her.*

Shawntriece wasn't interested in having a man, but she enjoyed being pampered. So, she couldn't help but smile and say '*thank you*' when Principal Powell helped her into his ride.

Companionable silence ensued as they pulled out of the school's parking lot and took off towards their destination. Then Shawntriece said, "I hope you didn't feel offended about the message that my cousin placed on that group of pictures that I posted on Facebook… You know, the ones from our visit to the science center. My cousin, Vivian, loves playing around. She knows goodness well that I'm not seeing anybody. I'm sorry that she implied that you and I were a couple."

Principal Powell shook his head. "Nope, I wasn't offended." He laughed. "Have you seen some of the things that my friends and family posted on some of my pictures? Your cousin's comment wasn't worse than anything my peeps have put on the Book."

"Good. I hate it when people try to link individuals together in a love connection." She sucked her teeth. "Everybody doesn't want to be married."

He nodded his head in understanding. "I feel you on that, Ms. Avery."

He paused for a few seconds then said, "Neek told me that Bria and Sierra's father is deceased — I'm sorry for your loss. By the way…is your situation similar to mine? I mean, you found the love of your life, and now that he's no longer here with us in the land of the living, you're perfectly okay with navigating through the world without a significant other?"

Shawntriece couldn't stop a frown from materializing on her face. "Sadly no, I have to admit that my situation is nothing like yours, Mr. Powell. I don't want you to misunderstand," she quickly added, "I loved my girls' father — he was my good friend for many years — in fact, ever since grade school." She shook her head. "But we didn't get together because we loved each other romantically. He was diagnosed with an aggressive brain tumor and given only months to live. He was the last surviving member of his entire family. He wanted to leave a piece of himself behind…you know, after he passed on. And as for me, I knew that I would never be interested in marrying and getting pregnant the traditional way. I happened to run across an article on cancer patients freezing their sperm for later. While reading that article, I had a eureka moment…I realized that my dear friend, Jason, and I would both get what we wanted if we contacted a fertility clinic to artificially inseminate me with his sperm. He'd get a kid to carry on his existence, and I'd get the baby that I always wanted to have." She smiled. "We lucked up and got two for one. Twins…albeit fraternal."

Principal Powell hadn't been expecting that. Based on how kind-hearted Shawntriece was — evidenced by how she was reaching out and selflessly trying to help his daughter come out of her shell — he couldn't imagine her not wanting a traditional family, complete with mother, father, and kids. He'd already seen proof with his own two eyes that she was a great mother. Instinct was telling him that she'd make a loyal and loving wife. *Why would she say that she'll never want a traditional family? There's something wrong with this picture… Something's not adding up.*

He knew it was very possible that he was about to step onto fragile ground, but something deep inside him needed an answer to why a beautiful, smart, vivacious sista like Shawntriece wasn't striving for the American dream. Plus, he wanted to know what was behind the pain that she hadn't been able to conceal in her eyes when she'd said she'd never be interested in marrying and getting pregnant in the traditional way.

"Why?" he asked.

Shawntriece knew exactly which part of her spiel he wanted an answer to. It was a very private issue. Two years ago, she would've shied away from talking about it. But not now. Two years ago, she had started an outreach movement to give encouragement to teenage girls who'd been sexually assaulted, and her outreach efforts had involved her publicly sharing her story — she'd shared it close to a hundred times. So, she was comfortable talking about it. The experience of opening up like she'd done had been cathartic. It had helped her release a good deal of her internal pain.

"When I was fifteen," she said, "I was attacked. I was raped by a grown man…a stranger. The assault took away any desire in me to be touched intimately." She shook her head. "I can't imagine *any* man in this world wanting to be in the type of relationship that I can give. So, I accept the fact that I'm gonna be single. And I'm grateful that modern medicine allowed a way for me to be a mother — like I've always wanted to be, ever since I was little. I'm happy I have my girls."

Principal Powell felt several emotions at the same time in response to what the beautiful, young woman sitting beside him had just said. Anger, sadness, sympathy — he felt them all.

He felt like stopping the car and giving her a hug; he wanted to offer his empathy and support. But that seemed inappropriate. Instead, he instinctively reached over and covered her hand with his own, giving it a heartfelt squeeze.

"I'm sorry, Shawntriece."

Normally, in situations like this, Shawntriece would say something like: *No need to be sorry… I survived and I'm thriving. I'm living my best life ever.* But the second he covered her hand with his, she felt every emotion he was feeling, and she saw every emotion play across his face. The sadness, the anger, the sympathy — she could literally feel how he was paining for her. The surprise caused her to close her eyes and fully enrobe herself in his offer of compassion.

"Thank you," she said after several seconds.

"You're welcome, and I understand."

And indeed, he did. He didn't know the details of the sexual assault — and even imagining it was making him sick to his stomach — but he could clearly imagine how such a traumatic event could scar a woman's life.

"That's why it's just gonna be me and my girls." She shook her head. "In your wife's passing, you have a situation kinda like mine — a tragic occurrence that just wasn't fair at all. That's why I can't understand how you still talk about God and all his goodness after a thing like that."

He placed his hand back on the steering wheel and let out a breath in a sigh. "When I first lost Yvette — my wife — I wanted to turn my back on God. I couldn't accept, nor comprehend, why he would take the love of my life, the mother of my only child. Yvette didn't die right away from the car accident she was in, she languished in the hospital ten days before taking her last breath. In those ten days, I fasted and prayed constantly

— so did three hundred or so other people who were in our circle of friends and family…as well as friends of friends. Despite all those prayers going up — all that fasting — Yvette still died. In my heart, I cursed God. Then I stopped eating or doing anything to take care of myself. I was so bad off that my mother had to take Shanequa. Then one day, while I was lying in bed, frail and emaciated, with my bedroom window open, I heard this lady walking down my street singing a tune as she strolled along. I didn't pick up on a good portion of what she was singing, but I clearly heard one line of her song. She sang: *The Lord said I am God. My will has been done.*"

He paused for a few seconds as he began reliving the moment. Then he looked over at Shawntriece. "I knew right then and there that God had sent that woman down the street to give me that message. Why? Because the latch on my bedroom window had been broken up until that day. I decided to give it a try anyway and it opened." Using his index finger, he pointed upwards. "The Lord wanted me to hear that message. I knew from that moment that I had to grab ahold of my faith. I knew that my walk in Christ would be strengthened and my faith could grow exponentially from the tragedy… That is, if I would let it."

He finally smiled. "And my faith has taken me farther than I could've ever imagined. I got the principal position at Higher Ground Academy practically out the blue — I seriously thought I'd never get a principal job, despite having the degree and being qualified. And the best thing is that at least three dozen people I've met have given their life to Christ as a result of me directly ministering to them." He paused and added, "All credit goes to God, but I'm happy that he was able to use me and my faith in Him to get the job done."

"But what about Shanequa? Due to losing her mother, your daughter suffered — almost immeasurably."

Principal Powell suddenly realized the reason God had put it on his heart to hire Shawntriece. *You're giving her a lifeline, aren't you, Lord? You want to use me to help her restore her faith. You wanna give her a second chance. She says with her lips that she doesn't believe in you, but I can see through to her heart. I can see that deep down inside, she really wants to.*

He turned his lips up in a smile again. "That's why he sent Bria and Sierra into my baby's life. That's why he sent *you* into her life." He shook his head. "God telling me to hire you was *not* a coincidence, Shawntriece. I'm amazed at just how much more my daughter has come out of her shell in the past couple of weeks."

"But I've only been on two outings with Shanequa."

He laughed. "I know right. I can't wait to see what the next couple of months are gonna bring. I'm excited for my little girl. She might morph into a little chatterbox, just like your Bria… Then *I'll* be the principal that their teacher is calling into the classroom to have a talk with his little angel, not you."

Shawntriece couldn't help but blush in embarrassment. Her older twin — by only a couple of minutes — loved to talk.

He smiled. "Yep, I certainly think it's possible, Ms. Avery."

She looked at him with doubt in her eyes. But since Shanequa really was a sweetheart, Shawntriece couldn't help but be hopeful for the little girl making a complete psychological recovery.

He laughed. "You don't have to say it… I know you hope I'm right."

Shawntriece finally grinned, "Yeah. I hope you're right. What are you, a mind reader?"

With one eye on the highway and one on his companion for the day, Principal Powell smiled, too, and said, "Apparently, but only when it comes to you, Ms. Avery."

She laughed. "Okay… If you say so."

Conversationally, the two fell into a very comfortable zone for the remainder of their hour and a half long trip to their destination. At the end of the day, the ride back home was similar. They discussed the events that had occurred during the conference, with no discussion of the prior personal subjects that they'd talked about on their way *to* Raleigh.

Shawntriece had left her car in the parking lot of Higher Ground Academy, so that's where Principal Powell headed when they made it back into Greensboro at a little past five-thirty.

All in all, he'd enjoyed his entire day with Shawntriece. So much so that he was looking forward to attending part two of the conference the upcoming day. He was even more surprised that he wasn't ready for their day together to end.

In a moment of total spontaneity, he glanced over at Shawntriece and said, "My mom's babysitting Neek. To make sure that I had plenty of wiggle room as far as time goes, I told her that I wouldn't be picking Neek up until around seven. It's only half past five. You wanna play hooky and do dinner before we resume our parenting duties? You said you like soul food…I like soul food. We can head over to Stephanie's — the soul food place on Randleman Road. It'll be my treat."

Shawntriece laughed. "I *am* in the mood for some oxtails…and some 'stick–to–your–ribs' mac and cheese — you know, the kind that only ya mama knows how to make?" She pointed towards the windshield. "Take the next exit off the interstate and make a left onto MLK Blvd. That's the fastest way. We'll be there in less than ten minutes."

He smiled. "On it."

* * *

Twenty-Five Minutes Later:

Shawntriece dug into her entrée seconds after the waitress placed the plate on the table in front of her and walked away. She chewed her first bite, swallowed it, and closed her eyes.

Principal Powell smiled. "That good, huh?"

"Yes, definitely. What? You never tried oxtails before here at Stephanie's? They're to die for…seasoned just right. A little peppery, a little smoky…all around delicious."

She could tell from the look on his face that he wasn't feeling it. "You don't like oxtails?" she asked.

"Never could bring myself to try 'em," he admitted.

"Hold on, wait a minute," she said. "You grew up in the South — in the boonies — and you never tried oxtails before? A country boy like yourself?"

"Nope. Something about the way they look or, how should I put this… They're off putting. And the name doesn't win them any brownie points, either."

She smiled. "They really are good. You're missing out." She pointed to his fork, while simultaneously pushing her plate forward towards the middle of the table. "Go ahead, take the little one. Give it a try," she suggested.

He shook his head, causing her to giggle and say, "Whaaaat? A buff, muscular, strong and strapping brotha like yourself is scared of a teeny, tiny oxtail? I don't believe it." She smiled and playfully pointed an accusatory finger at him, "The Bible says you should fear nothing but God, Calvary Powell."

"I'm not afraid of it, Shawntriece. It's just—"

She interrupted him with another laugh. "I double dare you."

Caught up in the playful moment they were sharing, he picked up his fork and said, "I'm a sucker for a dare." He laughed. "Been like that ever since I was in preschool and my bud, Henri, dared me to paint our classmate Antonio's fingernails purple during naptime with a colored marker."

Seconds later, Shawntriece could tell — from the look on his face — that he, too, loved the restaurant's oxtails.

In total 'I-told-you-so' fashion, she grinned. "See there. I bet you're really glad we decided to have dinner together this evening. Compliments of me, you just found yourself a new favorite meal. You're welcome."

* * *

Later that Night:

With his daughter finally in bed, Principal Powell sat down to unwind for the evening. He began reflecting on the day that he'd shared with Shawntriece. Just thinking about the fact that she'd been sexually assaulted still made him feel angry inside.

He was saved and filled with the Holy Spirit, but he was still flesh and blood. Accordingly, he found himself whispering under his breath, "I think there's an especially hot corner of Hell for people who do things like that…especially to children. That animal stole her innocence. He almost completely ruined her life."

He shook his head while thinking: *The devil is sent to steal, lie, and destroy.* Then he began praying: *Lord, please step into Shawntriece's life and recover everything that was stolen from her by that sorry-of-an-excuse-for-a-man. Please, give her peace, Lord. My heart is really telling me that you brought her into my life so I could help You bring her back into your fold. I'm your humble servant and I pledge to you my obedience in those efforts, Heavenly Father.*

He prayed for a couple of minutes more. When he finally said "Amen", he had a tiny trail of moisture on both of his cheeks. He was, indeed, an alpha male. But he wasn't ashamed to let the Holy Spirit move him to tears. He considered it to be his soul's cry. He loved the Lord. So, he understood that it was what it was. And to him, it was all good.

CHAPTER NUMBER TWELVE

Shawntriece woke up with a smile pulling at her lips. It was Saturday morning and she was looking forward to her outing with Calvary Powell and the girls. A whole month had gone by since they'd first shared what they now affectionately called their *Saturday Adventure*s.

The only annoyance was the fact that Calvary insisted on blessing their food whenever they ended their outings with lunch or dinner.

I really don't understand how that man stays committed to a God who could've saved his wife but refused to, she thought to herself.

Then she began thinking about other things about his character. She thought about how loyal he was. How kind and considerate he was. The fact that he was a man of his word…meaning he said what he meant and meant what he said and stood behind it.

"Yep, he's definitely one of the good ones," she said under her breath as she stepped out of bed and headed towards the bathroom, intent on brushing her teeth and washing her face.

She and the twins wouldn't be going on their outing with the Powells until later that afternoon. Shawntriece's mother had kept Bria and Sierra overnight and wouldn't be dropping them back off until one o'clock. That gave Shawntriece almost five hours of free

time to do as she pleased. Instead of housecleaning —
what she'd initially planned on doing — she was going
to have breakfast with both her sisters and get some
shopping in.

Less than an hour later, she was with her siblings
at a local IHOP eating sin food.

Angelique, the oldest of the Avery sisters, pushed
her long Senegalese twists back from her face and smiled
at her sibling. "I've been outta town all month, but I hear
you've been real busy lately, Shawny. Even busier than
me. Congratulations on the new job. I hear you're
working for a hottie—," she winked an eye— "and the
two of you been getting some time in off the clock, too."

Shawntriece graced their sister, RoShonda, with
some accusatory side-eye action. Then she looked back
at Angelique and said in a sweet little voice,
"Gee…Wonder who you heard that from."

"What?" RoShonda defended, sounding guilty. "I
didn't tell her you were *dating* the man. I just told her
you kicked me to the curb. That you've been spending all
your free time with him and his little girl."

Angelique nodded her head in agreement. "Yeah,
Shonda's telling you the truth, Shawntriece. I'm just
playing with you… I know you're not interested in
dating anybody. But tell me about your new job…your
new boss."

Shawntriece loved being an assistant principal at
Higher Ground Academy. So, she enthusiastically gave
her sibling the 4-1-1 on her new job. Naturally, her
conversation landed on her talking about Principal
Powell, too.

"I tell you, ladies—," Shawntriece said to her sisters, "—he's the best boss I've ever had. And I do mean *eva*. You hear me? Things aren't always perfect at work, but he's fair. And he's a decent person, too. He's so supportive of the kids at Higher Ground. He has a great personality. He makes you feel really comfortable in his presence. His heart's in the right place when it matters." She smiled. "Yeah, he makes the job a joy and not a chore. Hands down, my work life as a principal beats the one that I had in corporate America."

"Wow…impressive," Angelique said. "If all those traits carry over to his personal life, he'd be good husband material then. He's single, right?"

Angelique had asked Shawntriece the question, but RoShonda jumped in and answered with, "Yep, he's single alright."

Angelique turned her lips up in a slow smile. "How 'bout hook a sista up with an introduction to your hottie of a boss, Shawny? I ain't thirsty, but you know I'm in the market for a Mr. Right."

RoShonda busted out laughing. "Girl, please… You so thirsty that you over there drooling and you haven't even laid eyes on the man."

Angelique sucked her teeth and rolled her eyes. Then she, herself, laughed. "I guess I need to rein it in a little, huh?"

RoShonda nodded her head. "Yeah. You need to practice not looking so anxious. You don't wanna seem desperate when Shawny introduces him to you."

Shawntriece didn't understand it, but the thought of her sister being in a boyfriend/girlfriend type of relationship with Calvary Powell made her feel some type of way. Totally spur of the moment, she interrupted her sisters' back and forth banter with, "He's not looking for anybody, Ang. He lost his wife in a car accident a few years ago and he's pledged to stay single."

Good prospects were hard to find, so, Angelique pulled her eyebrows together in a frown and said, "Is that right?"

Shawntriece nodded. "Yep. He told me more times than I can count on two hands."

Angelique shrugged her shoulders. "Oh well… I guess another one bites the dust." She smiled. "My nieces got anymore friends with single daddies?"

Shawntriece laughed. "Nope. Sorry, hon."

* * *

Three Hours Later:

Right after hugging her sisters goodbye, RoShonda stepped into her car and pulled out of the mall's parking lot. She gave herself five minutes before activating her Bluetooth device and telling her cell phone, "Call Angelique."

As soon as Angelique said "Hello", RoShonda said, "You saw that I'm right, didn't you? Shawny *does* like that man." She hmphed. "The second you asked her to hook you up with an introduction to Mr. Hottie Principal, she was shutting you down…talking about how he wanted to stay single all his life—," she sucked her teeth, "—if you ask me, it's more like she's trying to subconsciously save him for herself."

Angelique let out a breath in a sigh. As much as she wanted all of that to be true, she had to look at the situation using caution. Her younger sister had gone her entire life without a boyfriend. The rape incident had robbed her of a desire to let any man near her. "I see where you're coming from. But I don't think that really proves anything, Shonda."

Believing that she was right, RoShonda said, "You been outta town on location all month, honey. You haven't been here watching all of this go down with your own eyes like I have. Our sister's got the hots for that man. I don't know how all of this is gonna play out, but I'm glad to see it happening… And you know why."

Angelique grimaced. "I hope this is one of our sisterly arguments that you win, Ro. It'll do my heart good to see Shawny with someone who can make her happy. I know she's not perfect, but she's a good person. And I believe that one breakthrough leads to another. If she can get past what that ol', crusty, no-good-excuse-of-a-man did to her, it'll open a space in her heart where she can actually begin the process of letting God back into her life. Know what I mean?"

RoShonda nodded her head. "Yeah. When I make it to glory, I wanna see all the people I love there. Like Grandma Rose used to say: *Being a good person ain't gone get you through them pearly gates.*"

Being a woman of faith, Angelique seconded the notion with, "Amen to that, sister."

* * *

"Mama! Mama! It's two thirty! Me and Bria are dressed! Time for our Saturday adventure!"

Fully dressed herself, Shawntriece stepped out of her bedroom and covered the short distance to her twins' room, saying, "Inside voices, please, ladies," as she walked along.

She grinned at her kids as soon as she saw them. "Sometimes I forget my girls are growing up on me… The two of y'all dressed yourselves without a lick of help from your ol' mama. Good job. But let me run a brush over your edges — it won't take but a minute — and then we can get going."

"You look really pretty, mama," Sierra complimented.

Shawntriece ran a hand down her jumpsuit and smiled. "Why thank you, sweetie. The two of you look really pretty, too."

The compliment made Shawntriece feel good. For some reason, it had taken her twenty long minutes to decide on what to wear for their outing. She normally wasn't a choosy dresser. But she was finding that to be the case over and over again lately.

"Mr. Powell's gonna like it," Bria quipped. "He said pink looks nice on you last week. Your jumper is pink, mommy. He gonna like it."

Shawntriece was sure that if she weren't a brown-complexioned individual, her cheeks would've turned as pink as her jumper on account of embarrassment.

"I'm not wearing this because I think Mr. Powell would like it, sweetheart. I chose this jumper because *I* like it."

You sure about that? Shawntriece frowned in response to the unbidden thought that flew from her subconscious mind.

"Come on, girls," she said, a little too quickly. "Let me get those edges so we can get outta here and not be late."

* * *

Fifteen Minutes Later:

Shawntriece drove up to the fifth floor of the parking deck closest to the downtown cultural center in which the pottery class they would be taking that afternoon was being held. She and her girls made their way out of the car, followed by Shawntriece taking each child by the hand. Smiling, she said, "Well, babies, it's only a short elevator ride and a slightly longer walk to the pottery class. We should be there in less than five minutes. Okay?"

"Okay, mama," they both said in unison.

As soon as they walked into the facility that was hosting the class, the three little besties squealed in delight upon seeing each other. Then they intertwined their arms in a group hug.

Principal Powell smiled as he leaned into Shawntriece's ear and whispered, "Didn't they just see each other yesterday at school?"

Remembering how she and her girlfriends were at that age, Shawntriece laughed. "It's a female thing, Calvary Powell. You wouldn't understand."

"Right." He chuckled.

When the girls broke their embrace, Shanequa surprised Shawntriece by running over to her and giving her a hug, too. The twins, following suit, did the same with Principal Powell.

The action surprised both adults. Shawntriece and Principal Powell locked eyes... Eyes that held an expression that said: *I wasn't expecting that.*

The three little girls then locked hands. Grinning, Sierra said, "We ready to go play in the clay!" She immediately followed that with a whisper. "Sorry I forgot to use my indoor voice, mommy," she apologized.

Shawntriece smiled. "Thank you for your apology, baby. Now let's get the fun started."

As Principal Powell allowed the women to precede him into the activity room, he eyed Shawntriece's retreating back in admiration. *She could've taken the opportunity to reprimand Sierra right out here in public. But she didn't. A kind heart...That's one of the many things I like about Shawntriece.* He began mentally ticking off a long list of things that he liked about the beauty. When he got to the end of his list, he tacked on: *And she's gorgeous, too. If I didn't know it was my state of delayed mourning causing this attraction that I'm feeling for her, I'd definitely think that I was falling for her.*

Noticing Principal Powell smiling away at her, a quizzical expression made its way onto Shawntriece's face, causing her to ask, "What? Is something wrong?" She brushed at her cheek. "I accidentally got lipstick on the side of my face or something?"

He shook his head. "Nothing's wrong. Just thinking about how much of a joy you are to have around."

She blushed. "Why thank you, boss. I think you're the cat's meow, too."

He executed a mock gracious bow. "Thank you, Shawntriece."

* * *

A little over an hour and a half later, they were all done with their class session. They had seven works of art to show for their collaborative efforts. The kids had completed six pieces. Together, Shawntriece and Principal Powell had done one.

Hesitantly admiring their amateurish masterpiece, Shawntriece rubbed a cautious finger along the border of the wide bowl they'd somehow fashioned from potter's clay. "Who gets to take it home?" she asked. "You or me?"

"Seeing that it doesn't exactly match the color scheme of anything in my house, I'll let you have it."

Overhearing, the adults' conversation, Shanequa said, "Nuh-uh daddy, we got lots of stuff that's the same color in our living room. It's the same color as the two vases on the fireplace mantel. And the picture of the sunset on the wall… It'll be real pretty on the coffee table!"

The piece of artwork really was an atrocity. It was unlevel, lumpy and literally leaning to one side. Not a showpiece at all.

Shawntriece grinned and stifled a giggle. "Is that so, Neek?"

Proud of herself, Shanequa nodded. "Yes, ma'am, Ms. Avery. It matches a whoooole lotta stuff in our living room." She looked at her father for confirmation. "Isn't that right, daddy?"

Principal Powell had no choice but to grin and bear it. Pretending to inspect the piece a second time, he said, "You know what, Neek? I think you're right."

Shawntriece laughed. "Since you get to take our gorgeous pièce de résistance home, I think it's only fair that I get something out of our Saturday adventure. Even though this is *my* weekend to buy us all dinner, I think my reward should be *you* treating *me* to a fish and chips platter, Calvary Powell. Don't you agree, ladies?"

Not realizing that neither of the adults considered the art piece to be a reward, Bria, Sierra, and Shanequa immediately nodded their heads in agreement.

Principal Powell let out a playful moan of disappointment. However, he didn't mind paying for the meal. In fact, when they'd first started their Saturday outings, he'd tried to cover the bill each time they went out. Shawntriece had been the one who insisted that he allow her to pay at least every other weekend.

"Okay, okay…it's four against one. You guys win." He laughed. "Dinner's on me today."

And it was a delicious dinner, too. They were tucking into dessert when they had an unexpected visitor. Shanequa was first to notice the newcomer. She jumped out of her seat and threw herself on the beautiful sista, giving her a hug. "Auntie Kat!" she screeched in excitement and delight.

The woman had swooped her only niece up into her arms as soon as she'd cannonballed into her. She now closed her eyes for a few seconds and held her close to her heart. "Hey, lovebug," she finally said, choking on emotion. Why? Well, the last time Kat had seen her niece had been four months ago — before the miraculous transformation she was now witnessing. Her deceased sister's only child had been almost non-responsive back then, mostly giving only yes and no answers, and only when spoken to.

Calvary grinned at his sister-in-law, who he didn't get to see very often since she was a sergeant in the US Army and thus stationed almost anywhere in the world. "Kat—," he said affectionately, "—tell me you're finally gonna be stateside for a while."

She laughed as she somewhat reluctantly set her niece back down on the floor. "Nope, I'm just in town for a few days. I was running in here to pick up a carryout plate… You know how much I miss the food at Stephanie's when I'm away."

"Aunt Kat, these are my best friends! Bria and Sierra. And this is their mom, Ms. Avery."

Yes, it was bad manners to interrupt an adult like Shanequa had just done, but Kat couldn't help but laugh anyway at her niece's rambunctiousness. It was good seeing her out of the shell she'd retracted into after her mother had died.

Principal Powell chuckled. "I guess my pumpkin kinda beat me to making the introductions. But yes, this is Shawntriece Avery — she's my new assistant principal at Higher Ground. And these are her two lovely, smart daughters, Bria and Sierra." Then motioning with his hands, he added, "Shawntriece, Bria, Sierra…this is Neek's aunt, Katrina Patterson…aka Kat…my sister-in-law."

Bria and Sierra smiled and gave a wave hello. As for Shawntriece, she grinned and stuck out her palm to offer a handshake. "Nice to meet you Katrina."

The woman smiled. "Nice to meet you, too, Shawntriece. And friends and family call me Kat." Focusing her attention on the twins, she added, "You two cutie pies can call me Ms. Kat."

Principal Powell suddenly had an idea. "Instead of getting carryout, how about you join us," he suggested.

Shawntriece could tell that she liked Katrina Patterson. There was something in her eyes that was genuinely friendly and welcoming. So, she seconded Principal Powell's offer with, "Yes, join us, Kat."

Katrina pointed at the mostly empty plates on the table. "I would love to, but it looks like you guys are already finished."

"We always stay and talk…for houuuuurs," Shanequa quipped, eliciting a chuckle from her father.

"Not for hours, pumpkin—," he looked at his sister-in-law, "—but we're probably gonna be here for another thirty minutes or so. You know I have a bit of a sweet tooth. I try not to indulge it unless I'm eating out. We just started on dessert. I'm probably gonna order a second one for myself." He smiled. "The ladies are gonna watch me pig out and keep me company like they usually do." He winked an eye. "Hopefully they won't laugh at me this time."

Kat grinned. "Okay, I'll bring my carryout tray over. Or better yet, I'll get 'em to bring me a real plate."

* * *

Later That Night:

Principal Powell was finally getting ready for bed at home when his cell phone began ringing. He smiled when he realized it was his sister-in-law calling.

"Hey, Kat," he said as his Bluetooth picked up the call.

"Hey, again, yourself, brother dear. Now that we're talking in private, you can tell me all about how your romance with the lovely Ms. Avery started. Man, you don't know how glad I am that you didn't let my sister down. You had me scared for a minute there. But you're pulling a last second Hail Mary."

Principal Powell knew exactly what his sister-in-law was referring to. On her deathbed, his wife had made him promise that he would find happiness again — that he would get remarried after she was gone. Wanting to do or say anything to please his beloved, Principal Powell had assured his Yvette that he would do just that. Find a lovely, kind-hearted, God-fearing woman to be his wife and Shanequa's mother. Get remarried. He frowned and went quiet.

Misunderstanding his lack of response, Kat giggled. "Don't worry, bro… I like her. She and her daughters have been so good for Neek — it's practically a miracle. And it does my heart good to see the love shining in your eyes when you look at Shawntriece."

His frown deepened. *Incomplete grief or not, I'm falling for her. It was obviously written all over my face. So much so that Kat could see it.*

"Calvary? You okay over there?"

"Yeah, I'm okay. Just for the record, Shawntriece and I aren't in a relationship."

"But you wanna be, don't you?" She'd asked a question, but it sounded more like a statement of a fact when it fell from her lips.

"I have strong feelings for her — I gotta admit that I'm attracted to her. According to Zay, it's just a natural progression of things. I'm completing the mourning process…you know, from losing Yvette. Nothing serious is gonna pop off between me and Ms. Avery."

She started laughing into her phone, so hard that her sides started aching. When she finally came up for air, she said, "You can't possibly be taking advice from your brother. Sure, he has a master's in psychology, but he has *zero* experience in the real world when it comes to affairs of the heart…not unless you count all the cheap thrills and one-night-stands he's had." She guffawed. "Trust me on this, whatever you're feeling for that sista is more than delayed mourning…or whatever Xavier said it is."

Principal Powell had Kat's words on his mind long after they'd ended their phone call. Lying in bed for the night, in the darkness, he stared up at the ceiling. *Is there any type of merit to what she said?*

He still didn't have an answer to his question as he finally dozed off. However, when he woke up abruptly in the middle of the night, from a dream he'd been having, he was sure everything had been resolved. In his dream, he and Yvette were each standing on the peak of two individual twin mountains. Yvette had smiled at him and said: *Move on, my love… It's a good thing.* Then she vanished like smoke and Shawntriece was standing on the peak with him, smiling and reaching out a hand.

CHAPTER NUMBER THIRTEEN

Sitting in the conference room working on a budget revision together, Shawntriece could feel Principal Powell's eyes on her. He'd been doing that all week and she didn't understand why. When she would look up unexpectedly, he'd briefly make eye contact with her and smile. Like now.

"You gotta tell me what's up, Calvary…um, I mean, Mr. Powell. You're looking at me like you're hiding a juicy secret." She laughed. "Although I admit it seems like it's a good one. The last time anybody looked at me like that, it was my sister, RoShonda, and she was hiding the fact that they were about to throw me a surprise birthday party. So, what gives? Cause it's nowhere near my birthday."

Calvary…he liked the way his name sounded rolling across her tongue. Totally ignoring her question, he said, "You know, since we see each other so often off the clock — and I think we both agree that we're friends now — I think it'd be okay if we called each other by our first names when it's just you and me together. Even here at school. What do you think, *Shaaaaawntriece*?" He'd deliberately drawn out her name in friendly, teasing fashion.

She'd been thinking the exact same thing. In fact, she'd slipped up and called him Calvary more times than she could count. It just seemed natural when they were alone.

She smiled. "Sounds like a good idea to me, Calvary," she said, almost purring his name this time, teasing him like he'd teased her.

The way she'd said his name felt like a caress to Calvary, almost a little flirtatious. But as much as he would've loved that to be the case, he knew it wasn't. *After what happened to her — what that creep did — flirting is the last thing that would be on her mind.*

The somewhat troubled expression that suddenly appeared on his face caused her to ask, "Um… You have a change of heart?"

He shook his head and lifted the corners of his lips in a slow smile. "No, Shawntriece. I don't have a change of heart."

"Okay. Now, back to what I was originally asking you… You planning a surprise for me? Is that what all the secretive glances is all about?"

He'd tried to be discreet with the glances he'd been stealing. *But I guess not.* He decided to try to laugh it off. "I'm just wondering if you're gonna look so put together after your night with our three girls."

She pretended to groan. Then she laughed. "Like I told you, I've never hosted a sleepover before — and it's gonna be the first one that Bria and Sierra's ever attended. At least it's just them and Neek. Too bad guys aren't allowed, other than that, I'd definitely be enlisting your help, buddy." She pointed a well-manicured finger at him. "It *was* your idea after all."

"Indeed, it was. But chin up, Shawntriece… I have faith that you're gonna handle it just fine. You and our girls are gonna have a great time."

Shawntriece shook her head. "There you go with your faith again." Her words were slightly condescending, but she placed a good-natured smile on her face to soften the blow. Calvary brought up God or faith very often. She was more than a little used to it by now. She was starting to accept it as just who he was.

He grinned, too. "Faith is the substance of things hoped for—"

"Yeah, yeah, yeah… It's the evidence of things unseen. Hebrews eleven and one…I know the verse well. My mama had me up in Bible Study every week—," she laughed, "—and I do mean every one of them. Now, if we don't get back to work on this budget report, we'll never get it finished today. Then we'll both be working till late this evening — in other words, we'd ruin the sleepover." She smiled. "I'm sure none of our girls would appreciate that."

He chuckled. "I'm sure you're right."

They worked on the proposal for a little over an hour and actually finished it. As Shawntriece stood up and began preparing to go back to her office, she flashed him a grin. "I guess the girls are gonna get their sleepover after all."

Deep in thought about what she'd said earlier about faith, he didn't say anything for several seconds. Then he said, "Will you humor me, Shawntriece?"

"Humor you?"

"Yeah. Will you trust me for about five minutes?"

She shrugged her shoulders. "Okay…"

"Hand me your scarf please."

She laughed. "Hand you my scarf? Why?"

He reached out his hand and smiled. "You said you'd trust me for five minutes. I promise I won't do anything to hurt you or your scarf. If I do, I'll buy you five more of them of equal or greater value."

She untied the colorful burgundy and gold accessory and placed it in his hand. "Since you put it that way, here you go." She laughed again.

With scarf in hand, he said, "Good. Now close your eyes."

Since she'd agreed to go along with him, she figured it would be best if she didn't protest. She simply did as he'd instructed and closed her eyes. Neither did she say a word when he tied the scarf around her head — around her eyes, blocking her sight. Nor when she heard him moving around picking up things at the front of the conference room.

Finally, he took her hand into his and said, "Just walk with me while I lead you to the front."

Seconds later, when they'd made it to their destination, he said, "Okay, here we are. I'm gonna move over here away from you, and then I'm gonna need you to listen to and follow my commands. Alright?"

This all seemed weird to Shawntriece, but she said, "Alright."

Calvary smiled. "Take four tiny steps forward."

Shawntriece again did as he'd instructed. Then she stopped.

"Good, good," he encouraged. "Now, lift your right foot about a foot in the air and take one giant step forward."

"Are you for real, Calvary Powell?"

"Nuh, uh, uh—," he wagged a finger, "—you said you'd go with the flow."

She feigned annoyance as she blew out a breath. Then she laughed. "Okay. Raising my foot a foot in the air and taking one giant step forward."

Shawntriece followed his instructions in this manner for a couple of minutes, getting closer and closer to his voice during the process. Finally, she was right in front of him and he took the blindfold off.

Confused, she looked him in the eye. "Well, what was that all about?"

"Turn around and look on the floor."

Shawntriece turned around and looked. There were piles of books scattered there in what appeared to be an obstacle course of sorts.

"That's how faith works, Shawntriece. Despite the fact that you couldn't see, you walked all the way over here to me using my voice commands. Not once did you stumble on any of those obstacles that I put down there on that floor. You listened to me, because you trusted me…and you made it over."

Instinctively, he took one of her hands into his. "Things aren't perfect in life — there's gonna be storms and obstacles — things in our way. But we have to stand on our faith and trust in God. He will lead us to happiness and joy if we only listen to him…if we only trust Him." He smiled. "Faith is the substance of things hoped for, it's the evidence of things unseen. Like you said…Hebrews eleven and one."

* * *

The demonstration that Principal Powell had done earlier that afternoon was still on Shawntriece's mind hours later. She didn't want to admit it, but his little performance had affected her. *Faith and trust.* Those were the two words that kept popping up in her head as she worked on the final touches for the sleepover — which was due to start in exactly twenty-seven minutes.

It was the first time her babies had had guests of their own over, so, Shawntriece had to admit that she'd been nervous about hosting it. However, exactly four minutes in, she realized that she'd had nothing at all to be worried about.

The three little girls spent an hour and a half watching one of their favorite Disney movies in the living room. Then they retired to Bria and Sierra's large bedroom for playtime. They played boardgames. They played with their dolls. They built a city with Lego blocks. They combed each other's hair, pretending to be in a beauty shop. Then they turned out the lights and the whispering started.

It was approaching eleven o'clock, so Shawntriece knew all three would be knocked out soon —their normal bedtime was between seven and eight. Shawntriece made her way to her own bedroom and curled up in the comfortable, plush, rolled-arm settee in the corner. She replayed the videos that she'd taken of the girls' sleepover antics, which she'd already sent to Calvary.

Fifteen minutes later, she tiptoed back over to her princesses' bedroom, expecting them to be knocked out by now. They weren't. They were still talking. Without interrupting, without letting them know she was there, Shawntriece smiled and turned her back. She began retracing her steps, but something Bria said stopped her in her tracks. It was the six words Shawntriece was privately dreading and hoping she'd never hear either one of her kids say. In a pitiful little voice, Bria said: "I wish I had a daddy."

I wish I had a daddy. Those words came crushing down on Shawntriece, causing her heart to ache. Literally.

Shawntriece's father had died in a construction job accident when she'd been her little girls' age — six years old. The ache from not having a father in her life was still with her today. There was a dark, empty place in her soul that seemed to always yearn for a dad…even though she was now thirty-four years old.

With a heavy heart, she made her way back to her own bedroom.

Sitting on her settee once more, she whispered under her breath, "I thought my love would be enough. I thought I could make up for it." However, she knew — from the tone of Bria's voice — that her child was carrying the same hurt that she was carrying. She knew it had the potential to scar her life.

I gotta do something about this. I can't let my babies go down that road… It's too painful.

A half hour later, Shawntriece was still sitting in her bedroom searching her brain for solutions to her dilemma. The twins' bedroom had gotten quiet, so she knew the girls were finally asleep. She answered her cell phone on almost the first ring.

"I'm getting ready to turn in for the night, I figured I'd call and see if everything's still okay."

Despite her problems, Calvary's deep, baritone made Shawntriece feel relaxed. "Your baby's fine, Calvary. She and the twins finally fell asleep."

"I thought so. I saw the bedroom light go dark almost an hour ago."

Shawntriece smiled. "You were outside of my house just in case your baby needed you," she guessed.

"Guilty as charged. I know it sounds a little creepy… I hope you don't feel offended. It's just that—"

"I'm not offended—," she said, "—I probably would've done the same exact thing if our roles were reversed. You love your kid, and this is the first time she's left you to spend the night with someone who's not her grandma or her auntie… Believe me, I understand. You're a great father, Calvary." *He's the type of man I would choose to be Bria and Sierra's daddy if I had a choice.*

That last thought brought Shawntriece's dilemma back, front and center, causing her to grimace. "Yeah, you're a real good dad, Calvary."

It wasn't the words that she'd used that clued him in on something being wrong. It was the way she'd said them. Something in his spirit was telling him that Shawntriece really needed to talk right now — that something was laying heavy on her heart. Something was also telling him that a face-to-face conversation would help her share her burden.

Every protective instinct in him was being activated. He wanted to be there for her, so, thinking quick, he said, "Thank you, Shawntriece. But I don't feel like a good dad. Neek's stuffed bear, Mrs. Snuggles, is out here in my car. I didn't want to interrupt you guys, but it would make me feel a lot better if it's there with you if she wakes up during the night. I'm still out here parked on the curb outside of your house."

"Give me a sec to turn the alarm off and come downstairs."

Shawntriece was a very classy sista, so Calvary was used to her dressed to the nines at school —and she always dressed super cute whenever they went out on their Saturday adventures or to her mom's baking class. The Shawntriece that he'd just locked eyes with was free of all the glamour, but she was just as lovely. Her makeup-less face looked freshly scrubbed and soft to the touch. However, there was a sadness in her eyes that he'd never seen there before. A vulnerability.

Standing inside her foyer with Mrs. Snuggles in tow, he asked, "Are you okay, Shawntriece?"

She suddenly realized that she was tired of wearing the façade of the 'strong Black woman'. Not being able to give her daughters the security of having a dad in their life was really eating at her. Making her feel ineffective. Like she was a failure. Weak.

"Was the sleepover overwhelming for you?" he asked in concern.

She sighed. "Have you ever felt like you're failing your kids as a parent?"

That was an easy one. "I used to feel like that all the time after I first lost Yvette and nothing anyone could do would get Neek to communicate like a child her age normally does. It's gotten better through the years — especially so now that you, Bria, and Sierra have come into our lives — and she's blossoming."

The fact that he was starting to fall in love with Shawntriece made him want to confess something that he'd thought he'd never admit. Something he thought he'd never tell another soul. He said, "And since I haven't remarried, I've been feeling like I'm gonna rob my baby of the opportunity to have a mother. In fact, she told me the other day that she wants a mom here on Earth like all the other kids in her class have."

Shawntriece was surprised to hear him say that. "You feel that way, too?"

"Yes," he admitted.

Shawntriece chalked it up to misplaced emotions, but she suddenly felt the sting of tears behind her eyelids. Then she felt moisture on her cheeks as the tears escaped their confines.

The decidedly masculine scent of cedar and warm amber tickled her nostrils as she felt herself being enveloped in a pair of strong arms. Any other day, Shawntriece would've pulled back and told Calvary that the hug was unnecessary. But every part of her being was screaming that she needed his strength. She wanted his comfort. All of it. She sunk her head into his broad shoulder and quietly sobbed.

Calvary realized that words were not needed…not at the moment. They stayed connected like that for close to three minutes, but neither of them was counting the seconds as time ticked away. Calvary fully intended to be there in that foyer, with his arms protectively around Shawntriece, for as long as she needed him.

Emotionally depleted, Shawntriece finally took a deep breath and pulled out of the circle of his protection, however, staying only a few inches away. Without making eye contact, she dropped her chin on her own chest. "Sorry," she whispered.

Calvary reached over and placed his thumb under her chin. He used it to gently tilt her head upward so he could see her beautiful, brown eyes. He shook his head. "Don't be sorry… You're a great mother, and being a single parent is a hard job. And you have two kids to my one, so I can't help but assume that it would be even more difficult for you, as compared to me. We all need a shoulder to cry on sometimes." Using his thumb, he brushed at the tear that was on her cheek. "I'm just glad I was able to be here for you, girl."

He wanted to tell her that he was also happy to be there for her because he loved her. But he knew that now wasn't the right time to admit that — he'd just now fully realized it himself. Instead, he said, "You, me, and our three girls…we've been spending a lot of quality time together over the past couple of months." He brushed at another tear and slowly lifted his lips in an encouraging smile. "You and the twins are starting to feel like part of my family. I take care of family, Shawntriece. I like to make sure that they're all good, that they're okay." He paused for but a few seconds, then said, "Don't be sorry, sweetheart. Everything's alright."

The genuine sincerity that she saw in his eyes — and something else in his eyes that Shawntriece couldn't quite put a finger on — convinced her that he was being truthful about all he'd just said. *He genuinely cares about me, about us — me and my babies.*

Emotionally, she finally began to turn the corner. "I must look a mess," she said, right before she displayed a sheepish, embarrassed little smile.

"Yeah, you do," he jokingly admitted. "But you're still cute as a button…you're beautiful…inside and out."

He said I'm beautiful. Shawntriece had heard plenty of men tell her that before, but she hadn't paid them any attention. Why? Because to her ears, it had sounded cheap and artificial. But not coming from Calvary. She could tell that he really meant it.

Shawntriece experienced a first that evening. That Friday night was the first time she'd ever blushed from a compliment that a member of the opposite sex had given her. She was surprised to realize she liked it.

Not really knowing the best way to respond, she gave him a shy little smile and a simple thank you.

* * *

Two Hours Later:

Shawntriece yawned as she laid her head back on her bed pillow. Calvary had just left five minutes ago. After their emotional interaction, they'd decided to watch a late-night movie together in her living room. Sitting on opposite corners of her brightly patterned, comfortable sofa, they'd treated themselves to microwaved popcorn and a viewing of the classic Tupac/Janice Jackson film, *Poetic Justice.*

Shawntriece began reflecting on her night. She hadn't been expecting to break down like she'd done in front of Calvary. But she realized that she was happy that he'd been there for her. *He's a true friend,* she thought to herself. *He has a heart the size of Texas.* She wasn't even upset that he'd insisted on praying for her before they'd parted ways for the night.

"He really *is* a great father to Shanequa," she whispered under her breath as a picture of his smiling face appeared before her mind's eye. Then she began recalling how patient and loving he was with his little girl. "My kids need a great dad like him in their lives."

She brought her eyebrows together like she always did whenever she entered a mode of deep thought and/or concentration. The thought she was having was singular: *I want Calvary to be my kid's dad.*

Lying there in bed, the more she thought about it, the more it seemed like it was a great idea. *He's single and never wants to fall in love again. I'm single and I'm definitely not letting no man get close to me. We could have an old-fashioned marriage of convenience. Separate bedrooms, of course. Strictly platonic. It'd be a win-win situation. Shanequa would get a mother — me. My babies would get a dad — him.*

She was convinced that her idea would be the best course of action for both their little families. Now all she had to figure out was how to make it happen.

Is it even possible? That's what she asked herself as she began thinking of ways to bring her new dream into fruition. Shawntriece was the type of person who was willing to fight tooth and nail for the things she really wanted. So, she was confident that she'd somehow, some way make it happen.

Lord, help a sista out. She frowned as the wayward prayer forged its way from the recesses of her mind. Then she surprised herself by smiling and whispering, "That's just Calvary talking. Obviously, I'm spending too much time with the man."

She closed her eyes for a few seconds, then opened them and stared up at the ceiling in her darkened bedroom. She began thinking about how much she had enjoyed praying as a child. How good she used to feel when she used to call on the name of Jesus and talk to the Lord. She suddenly had a yearning for that feeling once again.

"Father, God…" she whispered, while something deep down inside of herself was hoping that she'd hear Him answer. She suddenly grimaced. "No, I'm just being silly," she reprimanded.

* * *

As he navigated the mostly empty city streets, making his way home at one o'clock, Calvary still had Shawntriece on his mind. After the closing credits for the movie had started rolling, he had realized that he didn't want to leave. Sitting on her sofa together during the show, they'd been a good three or four feet apart. The entire time, Calvary had felt the urge to breach the distance and pull her into his arms.

He had offered her a shoulder to cry on earlier that night. Now he was realizing that one hug would never be enough for him. He wanted to embrace Shawntriece forever. He wanted to offer her his heart.

CHAPTER NUMBER FOURTEEN

"You wanna do what?" RoShonda asked in complete surprise.

RoShonda preferred early morning church service, so, she was now out of church and sitting in a tufted leather booth in one of her favorite chic restaurants — Blue Moon — having Sunday morning brunch with Shawntriece.

Shawntriece repeated herself. "I want to get married… To Calvary."

RoShonda blinked her eyes several times in amazement. Then she smiled and pointed an accusatory finger. "I knew you were falling for him. I told Angelique that you were. That's wonderful, sweetie!" She gave her sister a warm, excited hug.

Shawntriece slowly pulled herself out of her sibling's embrace. "No, you're misunderstanding me, hon. I'm not falling for him. I want him to be Bria and Sierra's father. And I'd be Neek's mother. It would be a marriage of convenience…one that all of our kids would benefit from."

RoShonda looked at Shawntriece like she had suddenly grown two heads. "Really? You can't be serious, Shawny."

"Yeah, I am."

"And you think that Calvary is just gonna go along with what you're planning?"

Shawntriece grimaced. "I don't know what he's gonna do. But I know what *I'm* gonna do… I'm gonna prepare my case and present it to him. Like I said, our three daughters would be the winners in this. Neither one of us are interested in looking for love… We'd might as well give our kids the best we can offer." Her frown deepened. "You know for a fact how painful it was for us growing up without Daddy. I know you remember the conversations we used to have. The yearning. The talks about what-if-he-had-survived."

Indeed, RoShonda remembered all of that. She let a breath out in a sad sounding sigh. "All I can say is that I'm gonna be praying for you, Shawny. Whatever way this all plays out, good luck, honey."

Shawntriece finally smiled. "Thanks, Shonda. I'm gonna need all the prayers and well wishes I can get. I've got to make this happen. I refuse to let history repeat itself again in this way in our family."

"Prayers?" RoShonda asked in disbelief. "You're okay with somebody praying for you?"

Without looking up from her plate, Shawntriece shrugged her shoulders. "I'm desperate. If somebody wants to pray for me, it ain't no sweat off my back. And if it works, then great."

RoShonda felt a song in her soul. To anyone on the outside looking in, Shawntriece's words would've seemed trivial...even condescending. But RoShonda wasn't an outsider. She understood the significance of Shawntriece allowing someone to pray on her behalf. *You have to be a believer to even want somebody to go before God in your favor. Lord, you said in your word that if we have faith the size of a mustard seed… I think this a sign that my sister has at least half that amount.*

RoShonda had to fight the urge to get up and do a praise dance. Instead, she simply smiled.

The section of the restaurant that Shawntriece and RoShonda were sitting in consisted of back-to-back booths that were almost ceiling height. As the two sisters talked, an unseen female occupant of the booth that was attached to theirs raised her eyebrows in disgust and disbelief. Done with her meal, she left a one-dollar tip on the table for her waitress. Then she collected her purse and made her way to the exit doors, making sure to take the path that would keep her out of Shawntriece's line of vision.

She frowned as she pulled out of the restaurant's parking lot.

* * *

An Hour Later:

Tasha had worked as a medical billing specialist in the doctor's office that Calvary's wife, Yvette, had been a nurse in. Calvary, Yvette, and Tasha had also attended the same church every Sunday — one with a medium-sized congregation, which allowed for everyone knowing each other. It was natural that Yvette and Tasha had become friends. Therefore, Calvary didn't think anything of him and Tasha still being on friendly terms. In fact, they now spoke to each other at least once a week — sometimes more, depending on what event was going on at church.

Despite their casual friendship, Calvary thought it odd that Tasha had just texted him: *Need to talk to you in private. What time can I come by your place?*

Sitting at his mom's house, preparing to have Sunday dinner, he texted back*: I'll be home today by 4. That good?*

See you at 4, she quickly replied.

Tasha placed her phone on her dresser and began looking through her closet. Winter was fast approaching, bringing its chill with it, but she wanted to look sexy for her impromptu visit with Calvary. From out of her closet, she pulled a burnt orange mini dress that hit her mid-thigh and hugged her more than ample hips. She paired the dress with patent leather over-the-knee boots.

She lifted her lips in a smug little smile. *I think this'll catch his eye.*

As the hour approached four, she pulled on her winter coat and made her way to Calvary's beautiful home in the burbs.

Calvary took Tasha's coat and flashed her a friendly smile. "Neek's in her room coloring in her coloring book. We can go in the study for some privacy."

She began following him towards the study, literally ogling his backside in his well-worn jeans as they walked. It was an understatement that Tasha was attracted to Calvary. She'd had a thing for him for a long time — even when he was married to Yvette. However, her respect for the couple's marriage had kept her from stepping to Calvary inappropriately back then. *But Yvette's gone now…and he done mourned long enough. It's time for me to step my game up.*

She suddenly frowned. *And I done waited too long, and now I got competition trying to step in the way.*

"Can I get you a snack or something to drink?" he asked, being cordial. "I have homemade pound cake and lemonade…made with freshly squeezed lemon juice."

She flashed him a charming smile and rubbed a hand over her hips, silently praying that he was noticing just how cute she looked in her little get up. "No, I'm trying to keep an eye on my shape."

"Okay." He swept a hand towards the sofa. "Have a seat. Let's talk."

Tasha was hoping he was going to sit down beside her. He didn't. He sat in the armchair, instead.

She pushed her disappointment aside and looked him in the eye. "I came here because I'm your friend — and I don't wanna see you taken advantage of. I don't wanna see you used and manipulated."

He was surprised and a little intrigued. "Taken advantage of? How? By who?"

"By Shawntriece…your assistant principal."

He couldn't imagine Shawntriece taking advantage of anyone. She had too kind of a heart for that. "Come again?"

Tasha had seen Shawntriece and Calvary together on several occasions over the past several months, and she could tell that he had a thing for her. But she was sure that after she shared her story, she wouldn't have to worry about Calvary being interested in Shawntriece anymore.

"Shawntriece is trying to trap you. I went to sunrise church service today, so, I was at Blue Moon

Restaurant having brunch this morning. I was sitting right behind Shawntriece — she couldn't see me because of the tall booths we were in — and I overheard her tell the girl that she was eating with — I think it was her sister — that she was gonna figure out a way to get you to marry her."

Tasha shook her head in disgust. "She's gonna try to play on your love for Neek. She said that she's gonna convince you that Neek needs a mother. That way, you'll marry her and be a daddy to those out-of-wedlock kids she got herself knocked up with." She hmphed, totally ignoring the fact that she, herself, had birthed her son out of wedlock. "You should probably even fire her. I don't know under what grounds, but I'm sure you'll think of something."

Calvary frowned. "You sure she said all of that?" he asked.

She nodded. "Yep. I'm positive…a hundred percent. The God we serve is powerful and He works in mysterious ways. It won't nobody but him who put me there in that restaurant at the right place at the right time. I don't normally go there cause they're a little too expensive for my blood, but I called the radio station and won a twenty-five-dollar gift certificate that could only be used at Blue Moon."

The look on his face told Tasha that what she'd said had just rocked his world. She felt giddy on the inside. *Yep, I ain't gonna have to worry about that Shawntriece heifer no mo'. That's gonna be it for them running 'round the city like they a ready-made family.*

Mission accomplished, she stood up from the sofa. "I know you thought she was a friend, so I'm sorry

I had to tell you everything that I just said. But it really is a blessing."

Because his mother had emphasized social manners when he'd been a child, Calvary stood up when Tasha did. She walked over to where he stood and gave him a hug. She pulled back and said, "I'm gonna let myself out. Call me if you have any more questions about what I heard, or if you need a *real* friend to lend an ear. You know I'll always be here for you and Neek. In fact, now that she's a little older — and now that she's talking like a normal kid — I'd love to take her out to do some girl stuff like manicures. Yvette always told me that if something happened to her, she'd love it if I looked out for Neek."

The last sentence was a lie, but Tasha figured it would help her in her bid to win Calvary's affections. *Yvette's dead and gone…it ain't like she's gonna be able to tell him that she never said that.*

Still frowning, Calvary nodded his head. "Okay… Thanks, Tasha."

Minutes later, Calvary found himself sitting on the sofa that Tasha had vacated, thinking about everything she'd just told him. He shook his head in amazement. "Wow," he whispered under his breath. "Just wow."

CHAPTER NUMBER FIFTEEN

After his conversation with Tasha yesterday, Calvary knew that he needed to talk to Shawntriece. He would be arriving at Higher Ground Academy within ten minutes to open up the school for the day; he and Shawntriece would be seeing each other once he got there. But from his perspective, their conversation warranted a more private venue than that. It was right after the bell for first period rang that he suddenly had an idea.

He made his way to Shawntriece's office and knocked on her door. Entering upon her command, he closed the door behind himself.

Shawntriece managed to give him a somewhat uncertain smile. After their emotional talk the night of the sleepover, she felt a little shy in his presence — even though it had happened three long days ago.

Wow, she's gorgeous. That's the thought that came into Calvary's head the second he laid eyes on Shawntriece. Pale pink lipstick contrasted with brown skin, making it look like chocolatey velvet. He knew — from holding her in his arms the other night — that just like velvet, her skin was soft to the touch. *Get a grip on yourself, bruh*, he reprimanded.

"Calvary… Good morning."

"Good morning to you, too, Shawntriece. As you know, Ms. Scott wants to take the second graders on a field trip to a farm on the outskirts of the city. Since the school has never sponsored an outing there, I'm leaving in about an hour to go check it out. I'd appreciate a second set of eyes…a second opinion. You up for a field trip?"

Calvary was technically her boss, so Shawntriece was well aware that he could've just waltzed into her office and told her to get her things and be ready to go at the appointed time. However, Calvary always gave soft commands, ones that made it seem as if his employees had an active choice in workplace decisions. Shawntriece appreciated him for that. It made working for him a pleasure, as opposed to being a drag. She hated leaders who power tripped and fed their egos by bossing people around.

"I'd be happy to tag along, Calvary. You driving or me?"

"I'll do the honors."

Less than an hour later, they were pulling out of the school's parking lot.

Pretending that there was nothing at all heavy pressing on his mind, Calvary said, "Our girls would be jealous if they knew where we were headed. All three of them love outings like this."

She laughed. "Yeah. You're right about that. Especially Neek." Thinking about the little girl who'd carved a place in her heart, Shawntriece added, "At the sleepover, she told me she wants to be a veterinarian. She even spelled the word for me… Correctly, too, might I say. That's a big word for a six-year-old."

Forever the proud parent, Calvary couldn't help but grin at that. Then focusing on the reason he'd brought Shawntriece along with him, he said, "My appointment at the farm's not until eleven-ish… That'll give us about a half hour of free time. There's something I need to speak with you about. Something personal. Do you mind if we stop at Barber Park so we can talk?"

Something personal? Shawntriece couldn't imagine what that could possibly be. Her brain then went into the slightest of panic modes. *What if he doesn't want me around Shanequa anymore because of my breakdown at the sleepover? He'll probably never be open to my idea if that's the case.* She grimaced. *And I haven't even had the chance to say anything to him about my plan yet, because I haven't figured out the best way to approach it.* She suppressed another frown. *I'm doomed before I even start.*

Quickly pulling herself together, she said, "Alright, Calvary. I'm okay with stopping by the park."

She felt her hands clam up in anticipation of what he was about to tell her. In her eyes, her babies' future happiness depended on her getting them a father. She couldn't think of a better candidate than the man sitting beside her. Not a single one.

He took the next exit and got off the interstate, within a couple of minutes they were pulling into a parking lot outside of the walking trails.

"Okay, Calvary…we're here. What's wrong?"

"Marry me, Shawntriece."

This is pathetic… I want a father for my kids so bad that now I'm hearing things. "I'm sorry… Could you repeat that, please?"

He didn't let his eye gaze falter. "Marry me. I've given this a lot of thought, and God put it on my heart to ask you. Like I was telling you Friday night, Neek wants—," he shook his head, "—no, she *needs* a mother. And you told me that Bria and Sierra need a dad. You're not looking for a real husband…and you already know my story. We have the power in our hands to give our girls what they want…what they need. It would be an old-fashioned marriage of convenience. We could live in the same house in separate master bedrooms." He smiled. "My sister loves watching house hunting tv shows…from what she tells me, separate master bedrooms are popular these days with married couples. It wouldn't be weird at all."

Shawntriece looked at him in disbelief, causing Calvary to suddenly consider that maybe what Tasha had told him was untrue. He'd thought about the situation for the last twelve hours, except for when he'd been asleep last night — he'd dreamed about it then. He'd prayed on the situation several times. No matter how he flipped it, his heart and his spirit kept telling him that asking Shawntriece to marry him was the right move.

With doubt meandering into the picture, he finally frowned. That is until he saw her slowly lift her lips in a smile, nod her head and say, "Yes, I'll marry you. What you just said…that's exactly what I've been thinking lately. You, me, and the girls having our Saturday adventures — and our other outings — proved to me that we function really well as a family unit," she said in excitement. Overwhelmed with happiness, she threw her arms around him in a hug. "Thank you, Calvary… Thank you for proposing to me!"

Caught up in the moment, she puckered up, intent on giving him a quick, friendly, kiss on the cheek —

much like the ones she often gave her sisters, mother, and girls. Calvary didn't get the memo on what she was doing. So, it just so happened that he unexpectedly turned his head to the side a few inches. Instead of landing in the intended area, Shawntriece's lips landed on Calvary's.

With wide eyes, she pulled back from him in shock. She stared at him for a few seconds as she slowly rubbed her index finger across her bottom lip. "Sorry about that," she said. "I…um…I—"

"You made a mistake. You had intended to kiss me on the cheek." He smiled. "I understand, Shawntriece. You weren't trying to lay a big one on me. You intend on keeping our marriage strictly platonic."

"Right," she finally managed to get out, almost stammering.

Oh, how Calvary wished the kiss had been intentional. But he knew Shawntriece by now. His love for her was genuine, so, he looked forward to the day that their kisses wouldn't be accidental. He looked forward to the day that they would be a real husband and wife team. He believed that his God wouldn't bring him to it not to bring him through it.

It's gonna happen, he told himself. *It's gonna be a matter of faith, perseverance, and time. If I keep loving her, she'll start loving me. I think she's already half the way there but doesn't want to admit it… It's something about the way she looks at me sometimes. It's something in those beautiful brown eyes.*

They spent twenty more minutes sitting in that parking lot, flipping ideas back and forth on how they were going to proceed with their wedding, envisioning how their new lives were going to be — how it was all going to play out. Then they headed to their original destination.

After they finally completed their tour of the farm and were making their way back to Higher Ground Academy, Shawntriece stole a sideways glance at her new fiancée as he talked about what he thought their girls' reactions would be when they broke the news to them. She was only halfway listening to him. Why? Well, her mind couldn't stop replaying the kiss they'd shared. Initially, there had been a brief moment of shock for her, but she was surprised to realize that part of herself had actually wanted to lean back in and kiss him again. It had been over twenty years since she'd had the urge to kiss anyone in an intimate type of way. So, she really didn't understand the desire. It was practically new to her. Foreign.

It must be because we're engaged, she reasoned with herself. *Of course, it's not a real engagement — and it's not gonna be a real marriage — but it's still gonna be one all the same.*

"Did you hear me, Shawntriece?"

Pulled out of her reverie, Shawntriece flashed him a guilty little smile. "I'm sorry, Calvary… What were you saying?"

He repeated his comments. Then as they sped back towards the school, they discussed how they would break the news to their daughters again. They weren't able to come up with a decent way of spilling the beans during their short drive, so, they agreed to talk some more about it on the phone later that night.

* * *

"You been blowing my phone off the hook all evening… Everything okay, Shawny?"

"Your prayers — um, I mean your positive energy worked, sis… He asked me to marry him! Today. I didn't even have to say a word about it. I didn't have to convince him of anything! I didn't have to argue my case!"

"What?!" RoShonda asked in absolute disbelief.

Sitting at home in her bedroom with the door closed for privacy, Shawntriece switched her cell phone to her other ear. "Calvary asked me to marry him this morning and I said yes. Don't get it twisted…he's not in love with me or anything. He said it's gonna be an old-fashioned marriage of convenience. Like I was telling you yesterday: Bria and Sierra need a father…Shanequa needs a mom. Problem solved. He was thinking the exact same thing."

"Lawd have mercy—," RoShonda shook her head, "—both y'all crazy."

Shawntriece laughed. "We're not crazy, sweetie. We just love our girls and want what's best for them. He's a great father, and you said yourself that I'm a great mother. Our kids are gonna benefit from that."

The sisters talked about the situation for a few minutes more; they ended their conversation with RoShonda reluctantly congratulating her sibling on her future nuptials. However, as soon as soon as RoShonda got off the phone with Shawntriece, she speed-dialed their big sister's number.

Upon hearing the news, Angelique's reaction was the same as RoShonda's. Disbelief.

Angelique shook her head. "A marriage of convenience?! Really?"

"Yep. This is the 21st century…who does that nowadays?"

"I know right." Angelique thought about it for a few seconds. "Wait a minute, a week ago you were saying that you think Shawny has a thing for that brotha… That she has the hots for him. You think it's possible that he feels the same way about her, too?"

"I don't know, hon…I've never seen the two of them as they interacted. But if she's going through with this sham of a marriage, I certainly hope so."

* * *

Across Town:

When Calvary heard his doorbell ringing, he assumed it was a door-to-door salesperson because they'd had a lot of them coming through his neighborhood lately. It turned out to be his brother, Xavier. He was returning a tool he'd borrowed weeks ago.

"What up, what up, bruh?" Xavier said as he handed Calvary his hacksaw. "Thought I'd return this." He chuckled. "You don't happen to have a level, do you? I'm trying to hang some curtain rods that I got for cheap online."

Calvary laughed, too. "You're a mess, Zay. Now that you've bought your own place, you're a regular ol' fix-it-man…but one without tools." He grinned. "I know what I'mma get you for Christmas this year." He began ticking off the tools his brother had borrowed over the last couple of months, causing Xavier to tilt his head, look at his sibling sideways, and smile.

"Hold up…wait a minute. You're in a mighty good mood, Cal. You're usually grumbling about me constantly hitting you up for—," he laughed, "—I mean *borrowing* your tools."

Calvary was generous to a fault, however, he *did* good-naturedly kid with his younger brother about borrowing his tools. But that was only because he was trying to get Xavier to be more of a responsible person. Seeing that they'd both grown up without their dad, in many ways, Calvary had taken on a paternal role in his sibling's life. After all, he was almost ten years older.

Calvary smiled. "Yeah…I'm in a really good mood alright. And I have good reason to be."

"Oh, yeah?"

"Yep. I'll go with you in the garage to get the level. Once we're in there, I'll tell you all about it. I'm trying to keep it on the downlow for a minute — I don't want a certain pair of little ears to hear about my news just yet."

Seconds later, Xavier was standing in the middle of Calvary's garage looking at his sibling like he'd lost his mind. "You got to be kidding me, bruh… I know you have a little thing for your hottie of a principal, but you didn't really ask her to marry you."

"Yeah, I did. And before you say anything about incomplete grief, I'm sure it's not that." He shrugged his shoulders. "Maybe it *was* the case in the beginning. But I'm a hundred percent smitten with Shawntriece."

Thinking about her, he grinned. "I'm sprung...that girl done stole my heart, little bro."

Thinking about the physical urges of the sensual nature that often influenced his own life, Xavier said, "It's been over four years since you've been intimate with a female — you know, had a woman in your bed — maybe that's the problem. I know you're saved and down with Christ, but I know a few hotties who'd handle those urges for you and not say a word...they'd keep it on the hush and you could repent later." He snickered. "Tasha would be first on the list. I don't know if you've noticed, but she got a thing for you, bruh."

In Calvary's eyes, Tasha Parker had been his wife's good friend. That's all. He had never considered that she may have been attracted to him. Even so, he didn't have an attraction to her. He wasn't remotely interested, and he immediately shared with his brother as much. In reference to the other part of Xavier's statement he said, "You know I don't believe in fornication, Zay."

Xavier grinned. "Right."

Calvary continued speaking. "And as for me wanting to marry Shawntriece for the sex... sex ain't gonna happen. At least not at first. I told her that we'd be in a marriage of convenience...that we were hooking up strictly so Neek would have a mother and her twins would have a father." He frowned. "Plus, I told you about her being a rape victim — it happened back when she was a teenager." Now angry, he added, "Being violated turned her off from wanting anybody to touch her in that type of way."

Xavier frowned, too. "Dang, bruh... I knew you told me she was a motivational speaker and that she started a movement for young women who'd been victims of sexual assault," he shook his head, "but I didn't know it had wrecked that much havoc in her life." When his eyes met Calvary's, the pain and anger he saw reflected there made him say, "You really do love her, don't you?"

Calvary nodded his head. "Yeah, I do. I've fallen hard, man. Even if it takes a lifetime for us to have a quote-unquote regular relationship, I'll take whatever she can offer." He finally smiled again. "I wasn't expecting it to happen, but God sent me an angel. He allowed me to fall in love again. He was — *and is* — merciful."

Calvary was still thinking about how merciful God was when he pulled out his cellphone an hour later and dialed Shawntriece's number. "Hey, Shawntriece…I told you I'd call. Neek's finally in bed. What about Bria and Sierra?"

"Hi, Calvary. They finished their homework and took their bath an hour ago." She smiled. "I think one of the first negotiations we're gonna have to have once we're living under the same roof is our kids' bedtime."

Living under the same roof…he liked the sound of that. He smiled. "I believe you're right."

"I guess you're calling so we can talk about how we're gonna tell the kids about us…you know, about us getting married."

"Yeah, I am. And I'm also calling to see how you're doing… Did your headache get any better?"

The genuine concern in his voice touched Shawntriece. It made her feel special that he had remembered. Smiling, she said, "It's better now that I've had the chance to come home and wind down a little.

When I get really, really excited about something, my excitement tends to trigger a headache."

"And us getting married is certainly something to really get excited about," he said, meaning every word of it…straight from his heart. "You and I… We're gonna be good together, Shawntriece. We're gonna be excellent joint parents…a beautiful couple."

Ever since she'd gotten the idea of Calvary being her twins' father, Shawntriece had been imagining them as a group of five — Bria, Sierra, Shanequa, Calvary, and herself. In response to his statement, an image of her and Calvary standing together as a couple appeared in front of her mind's eye. *I guess we **are** gonna be a couple of sorts.*

She felt slightly panicky as a result of her realization. Then she chastised herself internally with: *Stop worrying...there's nothing to it. You're not gonna be a real couple. You're simply gonna be a two-person team.*

She nodded her head. "Yeah, as for the couple thing, at least I won't have to worry about my sister, RoShonda, trying to hook me up anymore. In fact, I have two tickets to my high school class reunion for Saturday after next. They're burning in my pocket as we speak. RoShonda bought them for me… Said that if she got me a pair of tickets, it would encourage me to take a guest. My sisters and my mom were holding out hope that I'd someday date and marry." She smiled. "Now I don't have to worry about them doing that anymore."

"I suppose not. Class reunion, you say?"

"Yeah…class reunion." She paused for a second and laughed. Then she added, "I know I was just complaining about RoShonda buying me the tickets, but to be honest about it, I've always secretly wanted to go to one. Because somebody in my graduating class likes to celebrate every five years instead of every ten — like normal people — this makes the third one we've had and I've missed. Since I didn't have a significant other, I didn't want to show up at the reunions alone and have people feel sorry for me… You know, I didn't want people whispering behind my back about me being the poor rape victim," she confided, because she somehow felt comfortable sharing with him.

"I'm free Saturday evening and night, Shawntriece. Let me take you. I'm your fiancée after all. You should receive some type of perks from that. Let me help you make one of your dreams come true."

She really wanted to go, but Shawntriece didn't want to take advantage of the situation. "You don't have to, Calvary."

"But I insist. I wanna go." He grinned. "Do you know how long it's been since I've left the house to participate in an adults-only outing that's strictly for pleasure?"

She giggled. "I'm sure full-time daddy duties will do that for you. I have Bria and Sierra, so I only go out occasionally myself…and it's usually just lunch with my sisters while my mom watches the girls…or shopping at the mall. Nothing extravagant. All very mundane."

She smiled. "Okay, Calvary Powell. You got yourself a date. Well, not a date," she quickly corrected. "But you know what I mean."

He knew what she meant alright. But in Calvary's eyes, this would certainly be their first date, and he intended to pull out all the stops to make sure that his fiancée enjoyed it.

"Yes, I know what you mean," he finally acknowledged. Then he said, "And as for our girls, what do you think about us breaking the news to them this Saturday? After we take them to the theater and out for dinner."

As far as Shawntriece was concerned, the sooner the better. She didn't want anything to pop up unexpectedly and ruin her plans to provide a father for her kids. And the more she thought about it, the more excited she became about the prospect of being Shanequa's mother. Shanequa had really carved a place in Shawntriece's heart, and Shawntriece absolutely loved doting on her. She loved making her smile.

"Saturday will be fine, Calvary."

CHAPTER NUMBER SIXTEEN

For their Saturday adventure, Calvary and Shawntriece took the girls to a showing of the classic Disney movie, *The Princess and the Frog*. To say that Bria, Sierra, and Shanequa enjoyed it would be an understatement.

Sitting down at dinner at a local pizza parlor, the girls kept talking about the movie and how they absolutely loved the fact that the two main characters got married at the end.

Sitting beside each other at a circular table in the restaurant, Calvary's eyes met Shawntriece's. Then he nodded his head, causing Shawntriece to nod her head, too. She knew exactly what message he was attempting to silently communicate. Her nod was a signal that she was a hundred percent in agreeance that now was the perfect time to tell their girls about their plans.

Calvary smiled. Then to Shawntriece's surprise, he took her hand into his and loudly cleared his throat, getting Bria, Sierra, and Shanequa's attention.

"You okay, Mr. Powell?" Bria asked in concern.

"Yeah, daddy," Shanequa said, followed by, "Yeah, Mr. Powell," from Sierra.

Still grinning, he said, "I'm fine, ladies. You know how Tiana and Naveen got married in the movie, right?"

All three of the girls giggled and nodded.

"Well," continued Calvary, "Ms. Shawntriece and I are going to get married…how do you guys feel about that?"

It took all of a second for the comment to register in the three little girls' brains. Then all three screeched, jumped up from the table, and began hugging each other. The tears that began to trickle from Shanequa's eyes at first caused Shawntriece to be concerned. *Oh, no…we made the wrong move*, she thought to herself. But then Shanequa came over to Shawntriece's side of the table and wrapped her little arms around her in a hug and whispered, "You're gonna be my mommy…I prayed soooo hard that you would be my mom. God answered my prayer." Well, at that point, Shawntriece knew that everything was going to be alright.

Of course, Bria and Sierra absolutely had to give Calvary a hug. Beaming after their embrace, Bria asked, "Does that mean I can call you dad, Mr. Powell?"

Calvary felt his heart fill with love and emotion. He felt so blessed at that moment. "You certainly can, princess. I wouldn't have it any other way."

Shawntriece felt the tug of happy tears in her own eyes. The five of them were going to be a family and it felt so right.

* * *

Later that Evening:

Thanks to RoShonda's inability to keep a secret, Shawntriece knew that her mother and her only other sibling, Angelique, would know about her plans to marry Calvary before too long. Shawntriece's only request to her mom and her sisters was that they not tell the twins about her engagement. She had asked her relatives to keep it amongst themselves.

All three women had obliged. And now that the cat was out the bag, Shawntriece was dialing her mother's number to let her know that it was okay to talk about the engagement around the twins.

"Hi, mama… It's me. I just wanted to let you know that me and Calvary just told the girls about our plans to get married."

Janice Avery grinned into her phone. When she'd heard about Shawntriece being engaged, she knew a miracle had happened — that God had answered her prayers. The fact that her daughter was entering into a marriage of convenience didn't bother Janice one little bit. Shawntriece and Calvary had been bringing the girls to her baking class every other Tuesday for the past two months or so, and Janice had seen something that she knew her daughter wasn't aware of: *That young man has the look of love in his eyes when he looks at my daughter. And my Shawntriece is starting to have feelings for him, too — whether she wants to admit it or not. I know that everything's gonna be alright.*

Janice smiled even harder just from thinking about it. Then she said, "That's good, baby. Now, when are y'all gonna tell his people?"

"Well, we're gonna do it tomorrow after church."

That was a surprise for Janice. "You going to church with him?"

It was a surprise to Shawntriece, too. She hadn't stepped foot into a church in almost twenty years. However, when Shanequa had asked her to come to services with her and Calvary — and of course bring Bria and Sierra along — Shawntriece hadn't been able to deny her future daughter's plea.

"Yes, mama. I'm going to church with Calvary and Neek. I'm taking Bria and Sierra with me."

"Oh, okay, baby."

Shawntriece was confused. "What? You don't have anything else to say about it?"

Janice grinned again. "Nope. And on that note, mama's gonna have to hang up… I'm setting up the kitchen for the morning staff at the bakery. Let me know as soon as y'all finally set a date."

As soon as she disconnected her call, Janice couldn't help but break out in a mini praise break. "The yoke's been broken, Lord. You did it for me! You did it! Hallelujah! Hallelujah! I know my baby's bout to be free!"

As for Shawntriece, she placed her phone on her nightstand. The she grimaced. Just thinking about attending church services the following day had her stressing. Part of her wanted to go. The other part of herself — the part that had held animosity against God for almost two decades — that part was terrified.

She frowned as her cell phone began ringing.

"Hello," she said into the device after letting out a breath in a sigh.

"Hey, Shawntriece. It's me."

"Hey, you. Everything alright with Neek? She's not having second thoughts about us getting married, is she?"

Calvary could hear the concern all in his fiancée's voice, and it caused him to smile. "She's fine.

She was a little too excited about everything to get to sleep as quickly as she normally does. But she's in LaLa Land right now."

There were a few seconds of comfortable silence between the two, then he added, "That's one thing I really like about you, Shawntriece…when it really matters, you push your feelings to the wayside for others. I love your caring spirit, your big heart."

His compliment made her blush. Before she could respond he said, "I called to see how you're doing. I know the prospect of going to church tomorrow has probably got you all up in your feelings. I know it's probably making you anxious. I just wanted you to know that I'm gonna be right there by your side…every step of the way."

She finally exhaled. Something in her heart was telling her she could talk to Calvary…that she could trust him. "It's been so long, Calvary. I'm scared," she whispered.

Oh how he wished they were together in her home at that moment. If they were, he would pull her into his arms and comfort her…let her absorb some of his strength…reassure her that everything would be alright. But they had ten miles separating them. He couldn't wait until the day that wasn't the case.

As for now, he said, "God hasn't given us a spirit of fear, sweetheart — that comes straight from the devil." He sighed. "Truth be told, I don't feel like going to church every Sunday, but I get up and go most of the time. There has never been a Sunday that I didn't benefit from the message that was delivered in the sermon. Don't let the devil use fear to rob you of the word that

God has for you, Shawntriece. Don't let him win, sweetheart. He's stolen enough from you already. It's time to put a stop to it. You have a friend in me. We're about to be a family. We'll face this hurdle together…you and I. Okay?"

She still felt coils of anxiety in her chest, but not as bad as before Calvary had called. She took two calming breaths. "Okay, Calvary."

"Okay," he said again. "I'll pick you and the girls up at ten-thirty, that way you won't have to worry about driving. Remember, everything's gonna be fine. Can I pray for you before we say goodnight?"

Anxious feelings were causing a lump to form in her throat. Despite that, she managed to say, "Yes."

* * *

The Following Morning:

Nervous. Even though Calvary had said he'd be with her the entire time, that's how Shawntriece felt about her upcoming visit to Valley of Praise Tabernacle. Bria and Sierra didn't understand what was bothering their mother, but they picked up on something being wrong.

"Don't worry, mommy," Bria said as they got dressed for the church service. "Me and Sierra are gonna be good in church today. We won't talk when we not supposed to… We promise."

Sierra nodded her head in agreement, causing Shawntriece to envelope her girls in a group hug. Pulling back, she smiled. "I don't know what I'd do without you two lovebugs. You're the best daughters ever."

Bria grinned. "Shanequa's gonna be the best daughter ever, too. She gonna be our sister."

Shawntriece smiled. "That's right. She is. And speaking of Shanequa, her and Mr. Powell will be here any minute. We'd better get a move on."

"Okay," Sierra said. "But you mean *her and daddy*, cause Mr. Powell's gonna be our daddy."

Now it was Shawntriece's turn to nod her head. "I suppose you're right, baby girl."

An hour later, Shawntriece was sitting on a pew in the middle of the church with Calvary and their daughters listening to the pastor's sermon. Shawntriece didn't exactly have a 'come-to-Jesus' moment, but the message was one that seemed as if it had been written exclusively for her. The pastor had spoken on the importance of faith, even in times when it seemed as if God had let you down. Shawntriece was so caught up in the sermon that she didn't want the pastor to stop preaching. As she walked out of church that day, her heart felt lighter. She felt a tiny spark in her soul.

As Calvary took her hand into his and helped her into the front seat of his SUV, he smiled. "You just got some food for your soul?"

She grinned back and admitted, "I got a little nibble."

"Well amen to that."

Not ready to take it that far just yet she replied with, "Right."

That's all the admission Calvary needed. *Look at God... He's working it out already.*

Four cars over, Tasha caught a glimpse of Calvary with Shawntriece. Her mouth fell open in disbelief, then her beautiful facial features were transformed by a fierce scowl. She narrowed her eyes and shook her head. *Oh h to the nah… This can't be happening. After everything I just told that fool about what that heifer is planning, he got her up in his ride…grinning in her face like she the ish?*

Tasha wanted to go over there and confront Calvary. But she considered herself to have too much class to make a scene. She suspected that he was heading to his mom's house for dinner — like he did most Sundays. But she wasn't certain.

She stepped into her sporty, little mini Cooper convertible and began following Calvary's SUV, lagging behind to make sure they didn't see her trailing them. When Calvary turned down his mother's street, Tasha finally stopped following and parked her car along the curb. *Yep, he's heading to his mom's alright.*

She sat in her car debating on what to do for five minutes or so. Being that she was a friend of the family — and a close friend to Calvary's sister, Yolanda — Tasha knew it wouldn't seem odd if she dropped by unannounced asking for a plate. She sucked her teeth. *It ain't like I haven't done that before.*

She shifted into drive and headed towards the red brick, Ranch-style home on the corner lot.

As soon as Tasha rang the doorbell, Calvary's sister answered the front door and beamed at her friend. "Girl, you heard that my mama cooked Cornish hens today, didn't you?" She laughed.

Tasha grinned. "Yeah… Something like that."

"Well, come on back to the dining room and get you a plate, honey. You just missed the big announcement though… You ain't gonna believe this…Calvary's about to get himself married."

"Married?!" Tasha's eyes grew wide in disbelief. "To who? He ain't even seeing nobody." Then it suddenly dawned on her. She didn't even need to hear Yolanda say Shawntriece's name.

"Yep," Yolanda said as they walked towards the back of the house. "Cupid's arrow done struck again… My brother's in love, girl." She suddenly stopped walking and wrapped her hand around Tasha's forearm. "Wait a second," she whispered, so that no one in the back of the house could hear her. "You don't still have a thing for Calvary, do you?"

I was a fool to wait all this time to make my move. Tasha frowned, causing Yolanda to do the same.

"You *do*, don't you?" Yolanda finally said, her question more so a comment than a query.

Tasha turned her frown into a scowl. "He don't need to be marrying that girl. She only wants him cause she needs a daddy for her kids. I heard it straight from the horse's mouth. She was up in Blue Moon the other day pretty much saying those exact, same words to her sister." She shook her head. "That heifer doesn't love Calvary… She wants to use him."

"Are you sure?"

Tasha rolled her eyes at her friend. "Girl, please. Why would I lie about something like that? I even told Calvary. That's why I can't believe he actually asked her to marry him."

Yolanda let out a breath in a sigh. "Well, come with me to the back of the house and get you a plate.

You'll be able to see them with your own two eyes for proof."

Tasha shook her head. "Nah… I'm out."

"Okay, I understand. But call me later so we can talk about it."

"Alright."

As Tasha slid back into her vehicle, she had one thing on her mind: *Ain't no way I'm about to let this happen to me a second time. I met Calvary before Yvette did, and she stole him from right under my nose. I'm not about to let this new chick do the same thing… It ain't about to go down like that.*

* * *

Later that Evening:

Tasha was in a funk. She'd definitely been feeling that way ever since she'd been told about Calvary's engagement earlier on in the day. She'd now had six long hours to think about it. Anger, disappointment, grief, sadness, disbelief … she was feeling all of that.

She scowled at her cell phone. She'd try calling Yolanda three times. She hadn't answered.

When Tasha's phone started ringing and she noticed Yolanda's name on the caller ID, she accepted the call and snapped, "Bout time you decided to call me back."

Sensitive to how her friend was probably feeling, Yolanda said, "I'm sorry, girl. You know how dinners at my momma's place be. Everybody was talking, laughing, playing around... generally just being loud. I didn't hear my cell ringing. I just now noticed that you'd called."

"Right," Tasha grumbled in irritation. "And I bet y'all were up in there being nice to that heifer that Calvary done got himself engaged to."

Yolanda frowned. "Oh, honey…I'm sorry for being so insensitive. I know you like Calvary, and I can imagine how you're probably feeling right now."

Yolanda let out a breath in a sigh. She really did feel sorry for Tasha, but she didn't think it would be helpful for her friend to keep holding on to false hope. So, with a supportive, empathetic tone to her voice she gently added, "I think it's time for you to let it go, honey — this thing that you got for my brother. He's not feeling you like that, Tasha. All you're doing is blocking your blessings." She sucked her teeth. "Shoot, your Mr. Right probably done came your way ten times in the past few years that you've been pining for Calvary. Calvary was in love with Yvette…now he's in love with Shawntriece. You didn't see them together at my mom's house today. That boy is sprung…you can't win against that."

Tasha was angry. "She doesn't love him… I done told you what I heard her tell her sister at Blue Moon. What about that? And she ain't saved… She doesn't even believe in God. At Neek's birthday party at Chuck E. Cheese's you heard her talking about God didn't have anything to do with Neek suddenly becoming more outgoing. You heard her say that people need to stop giving credit to a mythical being for something that happened naturally or that man did himself. And I know you know she was up in church with us today —

probably cause Calvary made her come—," she shook her head, "—and she didn't even close her eyes when Pastor Heaton was saying the prayer." Tasha's scowl became even more pronounced. "That girl is a heathen and an atheist...downright demonic. You mean to tell me you want your brother and your niece exposed to that? She's gonna send them all straight to hell in a Gucci handbasket."

Yolanda frowned. She liked Shawntriece — she thought she was a nice, kind, honest type of person. However, she knew that an atheist would never have the ability to bring her brother life-time fulfillment and happiness. She knew that such a person would ultimately wreak havoc in her sibling and niece's lives.

Picking up on what Yolanda's silence meant, Tasha sucked her teeth again and said, "Yeah… I thought that would help you to understand what's at stake. Now what we gone do about it?"

Yolanda let a breath out in a sigh. "I'm gonna talk to Calvary and we can pray on it."

"Talk to him… Pray on it? We're gonna have to do more than that. I'm all for God helping us in troubling situations, but we gotta do our part. Like pastor keeps telling us: *Faith without works is dead*."

Yolanda frowned in response to that.

* * *

Across Town:

Shawntriece felt as if her Sunday had been an overwhelming success. Calvary's family had been accepting of her and her girls when he'd made their engagement announcement at dinner. Shawntriece believed in the old adage that said: *It takes a village to raise a child*. In Shawntriece's eyes, even though she and Calvary wouldn't have a traditional marriage, she wanted Calvary's part of the village to play a key role in her twins' upbringing. She felt as if it would make her three girls stronger, better adjusted, more well-rounded individuals. She smiled in response to that last thought. *Her three girls…* In Shawntriece's heart, Shanequa was already her daughter. She had always wanted a large family. The prospect of having another kid added to the mix was making her happy. And Shanequa was such a sweetheart…loving her was an easy thing to do.

As for her church visit, Shawntriece was pleased with that, too. For a second during the service, she'd felt that old tingle in her soul that she used to feel when she was in church as a kid — the one she had felt whenever the spirit started to move her. Standing in her bedroom in front of her mirror, Shawntriece stared at her reflection. She felt the trickle of tears on her cheeks before she saw them. Then she crumpled to the floor like a ragdoll and began sobbing. "I miss you, Lord… Oh how I've missed you," she whispered.

She laid down there on that floor crying, broken for a full ten minutes. When her tears finally started to subside somewhat, she had a singular thought on her heart: *I need you Lord… I'm sorry. I want you back in my life*.

CHAPTER NUMBER SEVENTEEN

She's changed. Calvary could see that there was something different about Shawntriece the second he laid eyes on her the following morning. She had a glow about herself — an effervescence — that he'd never seen coming from her before.

"Um, I said good morning, Calvary," she repeated as she stood in his office doorway grinning.

"Oh… Sorry, Shawntriece. Good morning." He smiled.

She'd gone so long rejecting God and anything that she felt had the slightest thing to do with Him — church included — that she felt shy saying, "Thank you for inviting me to church yesterday. I know it may not have looked like it, but I had a good time."

Calvary, realizing the significance of his fiancée's statement, was quiet for several seconds. Then he stood up from his desk and walked over to where she was standing by his closed door. He placed his palm gently against her cheek, cupping it. "Weeping may endure for a night, but joy cometh in the morning. I'm so happy for you, Shawntriece. Your night lasted a long time…but God has so much good still in store for you, sweetheart. Welcome home."

They both understood exactly what he was talking about. Shawntriece was happy and surprised to realize that she actually believed him.

The bell for first period rang, putting an end to the moment they were sharing. "I'd better go do hall duty for the upper grades while they change classes," she said.

He smiled. "Alright."

Shawntriece stood in the hallway helping the teachers monitor their students as they moved from one classroom to the next. The whole ordeal lasted all of five minutes. Then she made her way back to the administrator's section of the school building where her office was located. Passing the front desk, she gave the school's secretary, Mrs. Byrd, a friendly little wave of the hand. Since the school had an active grapevine — kids and adults included — Shawntriece was sure that the lovable, yet stern, middle-aged woman — who practically treated Calvary as one of her own family members — had heard about their engagement. All Shawntriece could think about right now was the fact that on her second day as assistant principal, she'd told Mrs. Byrd that she had no interest in Calvary…that she wasn't gonna chase after him like half the single — and some of the not-so-single — women who came to the school, parents and employees alike, had done. Shawntriece knew that she and Calvary weren't going to have a real marriage, but she also knew that Mrs. Byrd and most of the rest of the world weren't privy of that fact. Accordingly, she didn't know how the woman would feel about their engagement. However, Shawntriece hoped that she was okay with it because she actually liked Mrs. Byrd and didn't want to have a strained relationship in a workplace that she enjoyed.

Mrs. Byrd's eyes met Shawntriece's. "Ms. Avery—," she said, "—word in the hallways is that you and Calvary about to get yourselves hitched."

Here we go. Shawntriece lifted her lips in a smile. "Yes, ma'am… We're engaged."

Mrs. Byrd was quiet for a few seconds, which gave Shawntriece enough time to think: *Oh, Lord…she about to have a conniption up in here.* However, the woman nodded her head and said, "Bout time he found a wife for himself and a mama for that little girl of his… Congratulations." She chuckled. "The first day you stepped foot in here for your job, I told myself: *Self, now them two would make a real fine couple.*"

Recalling the first conversation she'd had with Mrs. Byrd on her second day of work, Shawntriece had a hard time believing that. However, since she liked Mrs. Byrd, as well as respected her, she decided to just let sleeping dogs lie.

Shawntriece smiled. "Thank you, Mrs. Byrd."

"Well, when's the wedding? And where's yo ring?"

Shawntriece didn't have an answer for either of those questions. She and Calvary had decided that they wanted to be married as soon as possible, but they hadn't yet set a firm date. And as for the ring, Shawntriece didn't even want one of those. In her eyes, a ring should be reserved for real marriages.

As Shawntriece stood there in front of Mrs. Byrd at an unusual loss for words, she wasn't expecting Calvary to come in for the save.

Realizing that his fiancée wanted to present themselves to the world as a legitimate couple for the sake of their kids, he came up behind her and wrapped an arm around her waist. Then he looked Mrs. Byrd in the eye and said, "When love strikes, sometimes a man asks a woman to marry him totally spur of the moment, Mrs. Byrd." Looking Shawntriece deeply in the eyes, he took her hand into his and kissed it. "I'll have a ring on this pretty little finger before too long and we'll give everybody a date."

Shawntriece was unprepared for the delicious feeling of warmth that she felt when he placed his lips on the flesh of her hand. She was even less prepared to feel her heart skip a beat in her chest.

"Right, sweetheart?" he asked, in what sounded like a sensual whisper to Shawntriece's ears.

"Huh — what?"

He increased the wattage of his smile. "We're gonna go shopping for a ring later… And announce our wedding date later, too."

"Oh… uh, right," she finally agreed.

Mrs. Byrd chuckled. "I see he's got you speechless, Ms. Avery. That's a good thing in an engagement…it's an even better thing in a marriage." She winked an eye. "It means that he done swept you right off your feet. Look atchu over there all in love. Glowing and blushing."

At that moment, the phone on Mrs. Byrd's desk rang, snapping Shawntriece out of her semi-trance. She slowly pulled her hand out of Calvary's. "Um, I'd better get myself into my office. I told Jonathan Klein's mother that I'd give her a call by nine-thirty. I like keeping my word to our parents."

"Of course," Calvary responded with a smile.

Shawntriece thought about the "kiss-on-the-hand" incident off and on that entire day, reliving the moment. She still had it on her mind when she got home that afternoon.

Why did I act like that? Feel like that? Those were the two questions she kept asking herself. And another thing was happening: She couldn't seem to stop thinking about Calvary. She'd be going about her day and then bam! She'd be thinking about some funny little thing he'd done or said.

She let a breath out in a sigh. *I'm about to marry the man. Maybe having those types of thoughts come with the territory…even for a "pretend" marriage.* Then she thought about what Mrs. Byrd had said about how to her, it looked like Calvary had swept her — Shawntriece — off her feet.

Outside of God and religion, Shawntriece had learned a long time ago not to disregard the advice and words of wisdom from the generations ahead of her. So, she was paying close attention to Mrs. Byrd's words, searching them for grains of truth. She suddenly grimaced. "Have I developed feelings for him? Romantic ones?" she whispered under her breath.

She was so confused right now…and everything seemed so out of control. A lot had happened in her life in the past several months: She'd barely escaped being prosecuted for a serious crime; she'd lost her high-paying job; she'd gotten engaged; she'd opened the door a sliver and was ready to accept God back into her life. *Now I might be falling for Calvary…a man who told me from jump that he wants a marriage of convenience. A man who's still in love with his deceased wife.*

The despair that she suddenly experienced from the thought that Calvary was in love with someone else overwhelmed her. It forced her to realize the truth: *I'm finally falling in love.*

Her pillow was wet with tears for a second time that week. The first had been when God had given her the breakthrough in her faith. Now, it was because she knew she'd never have the true love of the man who'd somehow maneuvered himself past all the defenses she'd had up for years and stolen her heart.

Ever since they'd gotten engaged, Calvary had been calling every evening to check on Shawntriece and the twins. Shawntriece was sure he was going to do the same tonight. However, she had no plans of answering his call this evening…she was too caught up in her realization for that.

When her phone rang at 9:15pm, she let it go to voicemail without even checking the caller ID. However, when she heard the notification bell, alerting her that she had a text message, she read her text. It was from Calvary and said: *Just checking on you. Sweet dreams and remember that God is a healer. He's merciful. Never let go of your faith, sweetheart.*

Sweetheart. Calvary had called her that several times in the past couple of weeks. Shawntriece had thought nothing of it — she'd assumed it was just a word he threw around with all his adult female relatives. Now, since she realized she'd somehow fallen in love with him, the term of endearment felt like a thorn. It brought her pain. *He'll never call me sweetheart and mean it in the way that I want him to.*

She swallowed past the lump of emotion that had risen from her chest and into her throat. *I know I turned my back on you for a long time, Lord, but help me please. Please help me to still be able to live with Calvary — for our kids' sake — without feeling all of this pain.*

After what felt like hours more of mental anguish, Shawntriece finally fell into a semi-restless sleep.

CHAPTER NUMBER EIGHTEEN

"Wow, honey, you got that big ol' rock on your finger and you're about to get a father for my beautiful nieces…why the sad look on your face? What's up with that?"

It was Saturday morning — five days since Shawntriece had realized her true feelings for her fiancée of convenience — and the pain of her realization hadn't gotten any better. It was worse.

Sitting at breakfast with her sister, RoShonda, Shawntriece frowned. She hadn't told another soul about her feelings. But she was tired of carrying the burden by herself.

Looking down at her chicken and waffles as she half-heartedly pushed the food around on her mostly untouched plate, she said, "I'm in love with him, Shonda… Do you believe that?"

RoShonda turned her lips up in a gentle smile. She covered her sibling's free hand with her own. "Yeah…I could tell that you were falling for him months ago, honey. I tried to warn you back then, but you didn't wanna hear anything about it. But y'all getting married…so you being in love with him is a good thing."

Shawntriece shook her head. "No, it's not. He's still in love with Yvette…Neek's biological mom. His deceased wife." She frowned. "You know he told me already that he only wants a marriage of convenience with me. For our kids. End of story."

RoShonda sighed. She knew that her sister had only recently recommitted to God, and she didn't want to scare her away from the body of Christ, but she felt she'd be remiss in not suggesting that Shawntriece use this opportunity to exercise her newly found faith. "Pray on it, sweetie. God really does want to give us the desires of our hearts. He'll work all of this out in due time." She smiled. "Plus, mama and me been talking about your situation behind your back—," she winked an eye, "—in the good kinda way, of course. She thinks that Calvary has feelings for you, too. Mama says it's something in the way he keeps looking at you when y'all have the kids at the baking class." She sucked her teeth. "Chile, you know nine times outta ten mama be right."

Shawntriece had a hard time believing that her mother was right this time. All she could focus on was how great Calvary kept saying his Yvette was. All she could remember was how much he said he loved her. She frowned again. "Look, I appreciate you trying to be positive for me, sis…I really do. But I think you and mama are wrong about how Calvary really feels."

"You're not calling off the wedding though, are you?"

Shawntriece didn't think she could bear living with Calvary on the day-to-day, while knowing that he would never reciprocate the feelings she'd somehow developed for him. But she knew she had to make it work somehow. As much as she now wanted to call off their engagement, in her heart, it wouldn't be fair to their kids. She and Calvary had promised them they'd be a family. That's what Shawntriece was going to make happen.

"I'm still gonna go through with it, Shonda."

"Good. And you're still letting him take you to your class reunion tonight?"

A sigh escaped from Shawntriece's loosely pursed lips. "Yeah. I suppose so. For whatever reason, Calvary's excited about us attending. I'd hate to disappoint him."

* * *

Shawntriece's mother was keeping the twins and Shanequa for the evening so that Calvary and Shawntriece could go out on their date to her class reunion. The reunion was being held in the event room of the Four Seasons. It was advertised as a night of fun, friends, and excitement. Shawntriece knew — from friends who'd attended in the past — that the party was going to be really nice — classy and tasteful. The theme of the evening was '*Autumn in Wonderland*', and the venue was to be decorated accordingly.

When Shawntriece and Calvary had talked about the upcoming party a week ago, Shawntriece had showed Calvary some of the pictures her classmates had posted online from the last reunion. Calvary had remarked that it kinda reminded him of prom, but in a fancier, more-adult type of way. Frowning at the time, Shawntriece had agreed. She'd went on and told Calvary that she hadn't attended her own prom because she'd still been mentally and emotionally recuperating from the sexual attack.

She'd told him that not going to prom had been one of her main regrets from her high school days.

Sitting in the backseat of a limo that was speeding along the highway towards Shawntriece's home to pick her up for their date, Calvary had their conversation from that day on his mind. He knew it would never quite be the same, but he intended to make this evening a substitute of sorts for the prom that Shawntriece had missed. Limo, corsage of her favorite flowers — yellow roses, bottle of non-alcoholic bubbly chilling in an ice bucket in front of him…he had it all.

Ten minutes later, Shawntriece had a look of total surprise on her face as Calvary hooked her elbow into his, smiled and began escorting her to the waiting limousine.

"Uh… What is all of this, Calvary Powell?"

"We're pretending that we're going to prom," he said as the chauffeur held open the back door, allowing Calvary to hand Shawntriece into the elegant vehicle.

Pretending we're going to prom? Shawntriece could barely wait for him to reclaim his seat in the limo so she could question him further about that.

"Well, what do you think?" he asked as he settled into the comfortable leather seat beside her.

She was confused. "Why are you doing this, Calvary?"

"Because you deserve for someone to do something special for you." He smiled. "I called Chauncey Miller — your classmate who was organizing the festivities. I had him to tweak the decorations to make things a bit fancier…you know, more prom-like. And I rented one of the private dining rooms that's next to the main event room… In case you get a little too overwhelmed by it all, we could go in there for some privacy.”

He couldn't stop himself from taking her hand into his and saying, “Your prom was stolen from you, and that was unfair. Like I said, I know this won't make up for it. But I'm hoping in a small way, this will balance the score a little.”

Calvary's words affected her. Shawntriece suddenly fell into her feelings.

“Oh, sweetheart,” Calvary whispered as he noticed the look on her face. He frowned. “I'm sorry… I shouldn't have done this. It's making you sad… It's bringing back bad memories.”

Shawntriece shook her head. “No, it's okay, Calvary.” She was somehow able to get control of her emotions. “I'm happy you went out your way for me this evening. I appreciate everything you've done.”

“Are you sure? We don't have to go to the reunion if you don't want to…if you've changed your mind.”

The scent of the yellow roses in the wrist corsage that he'd given her when he'd come to her door that evening hit her nose. The scent brought back happy memories of summers she'd experienced in the past…memories of helping her grandmother take care of her flower garden. It made her feel happy on the inside.

“I'm sure, Calvary… Thank you.”

Oh, those eyes…those beautiful brown eyes. That's all Calvary could think as he watched Shawntriece batting her long lashes at him in the dimly lit interior of the vehicle. He was sure that any other woman doing that would've been flirting. But not Shawntriece. Calvary knew it was simply something that she did when she felt vulnerable. Like now.

He'd been suppressing his feelings for Shawntriece for weeks — fighting his desires to touch her, to communicate how he felt about her. He didn't know how much longer he could keep his attraction to her under wraps. In fact, right now felt like the tipping point.

Now is not the time, he told himself as he fought the urge to cup her velvety soft cheek and whisper sweet nothings in her ear.

"You're welcome…it's my pleasure to be your escort tonight," he finally responded as he reached for the bottle of sparkling juice that was on ice. "I know you said that like me, you don't drink. So, I bought this bottle of sparkling peach nectar. It's spiced with a touch of cinnamon, and it's pretty good." He picked up one of the wine glasses. "Wanna give it a try?"

She smiled. "It wouldn't be prom if I didn't," she teased.

He grinned, too. "I believe you're right."

The venue was absolutely beautiful. Shawntriece could definitely tell that someone had gone above and beyond on the decorations. There was an ambience reminiscent of prom, but in an adult type of way.

As Calvary escorted her into the event room on his elbow, Shawntriece realized that only one thing would make the night perfect: *If only he were mine…if only we were a real couple.* Her feelings for him — a man she knew would never be hers — caused a pain in her heart. She frowned as she tried to fight the sadness that was slowly washing over her.

Calvary — keenly in tune with Shawntriece's feelings — leaned down and whispered in her ear, "That private room that I was telling you about is to our right. Let's go check it out."

Shawntriece didn't fight him. Being there with her classmates from one of the darkest times in her life — combined with the feelings she had because she knew Calvary would never love her — was overwhelming. They'd only just gotten there, but she needed a break.

With the door to the small dining room closed behind them, Calvary grimaced. "Coming here was a bad idea…you're not ready for this yet, are you sweetheart?"

The way he'd called her sweetheart did it for Shawntriece. She knew that the moisture that suddenly pooled in the corner of her eyes was going to ruin her makeup, but she didn't care…she needed a reprieve from the internal pain.

This time, Calvary couldn't stop himself from pulling the woman who'd stolen his heart into his arms. "Oh, baby—," he whispered into her ear, "—my beautiful Earth angel…oh, sweetheart. Everything's gonna be alright." He wished he could bear her pain himself.

Shawntriece had never been in an intimate relationship, but she wasn't a fool. She knew words like those were reserved for lovers. Knowing that he'd never fall for her in the way she'd fallen for him, she couldn't bear hearing Calvary utter such words in her ear. Her thoughts caused her to pull out of the warm, protective circle of his arms.

With her cheeks now wet with tears, she closed her eyes and shook her head. "Don't say things like that to me, Calvary. I...I...I can't take hearing it."

He misunderstood where she was coming from. He had no idea she'd said what she'd said because she was in love with him. He assumed the opposite: That due to her traumatic experience, she'd never be able to open her heart to love.

Calvary had known this day was coming — the day he'd no longer be able to hold his feelings for Shawntriece in check. He looked into her beautiful eyes for several seconds. Then he cupped her soft cheek in the palm of his hand. "I'll try my best not to say things like that to you, Shawntriece. But I have to confess that it's gonna be a hard thing for me to accomplish." He sighed. "I love you...I'm *in* love with you...and my feelings seem to get stronger and stronger as each day goes by."

She was sure this was another case of her hearing what she wanted to hear. She was certain that Calvary hadn't said that he was in love with her.

He nodded his head. "Yeah, I'm in love with you, Shawntriece." He took her hand and placed her palm flat against his chest, over the spot where his heart lay. "You've carved a place right here."

She was confused. "But what about your wife? What about Yvette? You're in love with her."

"I'll always love Yvette, sweetheart. But God is merciful, and he saw fit to bless me with you. He allowed you to steal my heart, Shawntriece. You blindsided me with your beauty — inside and out, your grace, your kind heart." He smiled. "How can I not love you? There isn't a day that goes by that I don't thank God for placing you in my life."

He frowned then continued speaking. "I know you've been hurt — traumatized on a level that I could never comprehend. I know you may never be able to love me in return in the way that I love you. But I'd rather spend each day of the rest of my life with you in a marriage of convenience than not have you by my side at all." He palmed her smooth cheek again. "That's how much I love you, babe."

She believed him. Every single word that he'd spoken.

The spark that he suddenly saw catch fire in her eyes clued him in on how she was really feeling. "You love me, too," he said.

"Yes," she whispered.

Yes. That single word was like a melodic chorus to Calvary's ears. The woman he loved, loved him right back. He wanted to kiss her badly. Stake his claim. But given her situation, he didn't know if that was the best of ideas…but oh how he yearned to taste her sweet lips under his.

Then she closed her eyes and tilted her head backwards. From that slightest of moves, he knew exactly what she wanted. She wanted the same thing that he did.

Shawntriece's first kiss from her fiancée was exactly how she'd dreamed it would be and more…it felt like pure heaven.

After what felt like an eternity of bliss, Calvary finally forced himself to pull his lips away from hers. If he kissed her any longer, he knew he'd want much more.

And given that they were in a private room, behind a locked door, he knew it would be so easy to fulfill those desires. But his love of God and the Word kept him from going there. And in his mind, his sweetheart deserved much more than that for their first time together.

Shawntriece blushed and gave him a shy smile. "Wow," she said.

He grinned, too. "Yeah, wow. I can't wait to make you Mrs. Powell… We have a life full of love ahead of us, babe."

She couldn't help but agree.

* * *

When Shawntriece finally made it to bed that night, she had a wide smile on her face. She still couldn't quite believe that Calvary was in love with her, but she had her memories from their beautiful evening together to prove it.

She opened her eyes in her darkened bedroom and looked up at the ceiling. "Lord, I know I don't deserve it, but thank you for all the blessings you've given me. In two weeks, I'm going to be Mrs. Calvary Powell. I'm going to have a husband and a new daughter — something I never dreamed would ever happen. And best of all, my boo is in love with me."

CHAPTER NUMBER NINETEEN

It had been two days since the class reunion. Shawntriece was positively glowing from being in love and being loved in return. She was certain that she wanted to marry Calvary. However, she wanted to touch bases with her therapist to check for any hidden gotchas that could potentially ruin her and Calvary's marriage.

There were plenty of people who placed stigmas on getting psychological counseling. Shawntriece wasn't one of them. As a result of being sexually assaulted, she'd come to realize that having a professional to talk to about troubling situations could be a beneficial lifeline.

Shawntriece only talked to her therapist every couple of months now — as opposed to every week like she used to when she'd first sought therapy decades ago as a teen.

As an individual whose first and only sexual encounter had been one of violation, she had valid concerns about whether she could face being intimate with Calvary. Every one of her instincts was saying yes. However, she needed a second opinion. She needed to talk to someone who was good at digging into the private recesses of her mind.

As Shawntriece walked out of Dr. Benita Howell's office that afternoon, she had a smile on her face as bright as the sun in God's blue sky. In Dr. Howell's professional opinion, she believed that

Shawntriece was ready. She'd even given her a list of bullet points she'd compiled to prove it. Since Shawntriece also considered Dr. Howell to be a friend, she believed her. On top of that, ever bullet point on the list made sense.

She'd taken a day off from work, so she didn't have to go back to Higher Ground Academy today. Calvary — taking on the role of father of three a couple of weeks early — was taking all three girls home with him after school. Shawntriece would be picking Bria and Sierra up from his place around six.

Wow… I can't believe we're about to be a family. Me, Calvary, and the girls. What a blessing!

That's the thought she had in her mind when she pulled into her driveway that sunny Monday morning and checked her mailbox. The only thing in the box was a letter addressed to her with no return address. Shawntriece immediately assumed that it was junk mail. However, the words, '*Open Me*', in handwritten text on the back flap stopped her from trashing it. As soon as she stepped into her study, she slit the letter open and began reading it. By the time she'd reached the end of the letter, she dropped her chin on her chest in a mixture of disappoint and anger. She suddenly felt dirty and she couldn't believe that she'd ever contemplated letting Calvary touch her…intimately or otherwise.

She sank into the office chair in the tastefully decorated room as hot tears began to sting the backs of her eyelids. After having a good cry, she sat in that chair, numb for a good hour. She frowned as her cell phone began ringing.

Seeing that she was supposed to have met RoShonda for lunch fifteen minutes ago, she suspected that it was her sister calling. She let the call go to voicemail. She was somehow able to summon the strength to text '*something came up*' to her sibling.

She glared at the single sheet of paper on the floor in front of her. She knew that two lines from the letter would always be emblazoned in her mind. Those two lines being: *Calvary is not who you think he is, he's a child molester. He's a sexual predator*. The letter had gone on in detail to describe how Calvary had worked as a high school teacher in a private school ten years ago, and that he'd propositioned one of the students for sex. The sender of the letter had also included a copy of a newspaper article from one state over — Virginia — that proved his or her case.

* * *

Across Town:

Standing in a downtown sandwich shop paying for both her and Shawntriece's sandwich orders, RoShonda frowned at the text message her sister had just sent her.

"Is something wrong with your order ma'am?" the girl behind the counter asked her.

RoShonda shook her head and offered up a friendly smile. "No, it looks fine. It's just that my sister isn't gonna be able to meet me here for lunch after all. I'mma have to get this in a doggie bag."

As RoShonda pulled out of the sandwich shop's parking lot, she glanced down at the two bags of food on her passenger-side seat and grimaced. *Ain't nobody gonna wanna eat Shawny's sandwich with that nasty anchovy paste and capers on it. I got her spare key…I'mma drive this monstrosity over to her house and leave it in her fridge, then bounce.*

As Shawntriece's home came into view, RoShonda was surprised to see her sister's car in the driveway. "Lord, I hope her and that fiancée of hers ain't up in that house playing hooky." She smiled. "But I can't say I blame her…being in love will do that for a sista."

She parked her car in the driveway behind Shawntriece's, then made her way to the front door, sandwich in hand. She rang the doorbell four times before Shawntriece finally answered it.

The joke that RoShonda had on the tip of her tongue vanished when she got a look at her sister's face. "What's wrong, honey?" RoShonda asked, well past concerned.

Shawntriece was all cried out by now. So, in a voice that was devoid of emotion, she said, "I'm calling the wedding off. Calvary…he's a sexual predator…a child abuser."

"What?!"

With RoShonda following her, Shawntriece walked over to the desk in the study located to the left of her spacious foyer. She picked up the letter and said, "Here, read it for yourself."

RoShonda quickly read the letter and the attached newspaper article. Then she looked up at her sister.

"See what I'm talking about?" Shawntriece asked.

RoShonda thought about it a few seconds. "This looks bad, Shawny…I admit that. But you had a background check done on Calvary the day after you started talking about how you wanted to hook up with him in a marriage of convenience. You went through a reputable company. They didn't find any convictions… You showed me the report. Remember? That brotha was squeaky clean."

Not waiting for her sibling to respond, RoShonda added, "If he had committed a crime — and was prosecuted for the said crime — it would've been in that report." She waved the letter in her hand. "Plus, this newspaper article says that he was accused of trying to initiate an inappropriate sexual relationship with a female student…the operative word is *accused*. So, we don't know how much truth was in the accusation…we don't know what came of it." She let out a breath in a sigh. "Now, I know — because of what happened to you — this is a sensitive situation…and I can only imagine how tore up this got you on the inside. But it might not be what you're thinking, honey. Bottom line is…you need to ask him about this, Shawny. Give the man a chance to explain himself. And then do one of the things you do best…investigate whatever he tells you, investigate his behind."

Shawntriece wanted to believe that there was some type of way that this was a huge misunderstanding — however, she doubted it. She frowned. "He's supposed to be taking Bria and Sierra home with him and Shanequa this evening after school…ain't no way I'm about to let that happen. I gotta protect my girls." Her eyes met her sibling's. "Can you sign them out of school early — in about an hour — and take them to mama at the bakery? I don't wanna run into Calvary right now, and I need some time to figure out what I'm gonna do."

RoShonda gave her sibling a heartfelt hug, then she pulled back and said, "Sure thing, sis. I'll head over there right now. To kill some time, I'll eat my sandwich in the school's parking lot, then go sign them out."

* * *

Across Town:

Calvary's sister, Yolanda, took the phone call that had been transferred to her by the switchboard attendant at her job. As soon as she realized that it was Tasha calling, she wished that she had caller ID.

"What is it, Tasha? You know I stay busy here at work."

Tasha sucked her teeth. "Girl, please…you got a cushy job with lots of downtime…with nobody breathing down your neck and checking over your shoulder. Don't try to play like you don't. It's me you're talking to, so I know."

Knowing that she couldn't honestly deny any of that, Yolanda said, "Well, what's wrong now, Tasha?"

Tasha smiled. "I was just wondering if you had heard anything from Calvary today. I know that heifer probably got my letter by now. I mailed it on Friday and her address is right here in the city. The lady at the post office said that it would only take a day…two tops. I know she didn't get it Saturday, cause if she had, she wouldn't have been all up in church holding hands with Calvary yesterday…acting like they already married."

She frowned in displeasure from the imagery that the memory produced in her brain.

Yolanda grimaced. She had quietly gone along with Tasha's plans to place a wedge between her brother and Shawntriece — that was because she didn't want to see her brother unequally yoked and married to someone who had no love for the Lord — an atheist. But in the past couple of weeks, that had all changed. Yolanda had even witnessed her brother's fiancée walk up to the altar and sincerely recommit her life to Christ — Shawntriece had done that yesterday.

"Well?" Tasha asked, not even trying to disguise the note of irritation in her voice.

Yolanda sighed. "No, I haven't heard from him, Tasha. And it's not like I was exactly expecting to hear from him either. He's at work, honey… Shawntriece is, too." She sucked her teeth. "If the letter *does* come today, she probably isn't even gonna open it until later on tonight."

Tasha frowned. "That's why I'm mad I took your advice and mailed it. If I had just stuck it in her mailbox — like I had wanted to do — the heifer woulda had it by now."

"Girl, don't you know how many people got security cameras? You said you were trying to stay anonymous…that you didn't want Calvary to know that you're the one who ratted him out. How is that gonna happen if she sees your big ol' forehead on her security camera? Answer me that, boo."

"Alright, alright," Tasha consented. "But you didn't have to be nasty about it. E'rbody know I got a big forehead…but I'm still cute."

"Right." Yolanda paused then added, "Look, Tasha…my boss just stepped in. I gotta get off this phone discussing personal business while I'm on the clock."

Five minutes later, Yolanda was punching out for the day. One thing she loved about her job was the nontraditional work hours. As she embarked on the drive home, she had the situation with Shawntriece on her mind. The closer she got to her destination, the more she began to think: *What Tasha is trying to do to my brother and his fiancée ain't right.*

She grimaced as she pulled into her garage.

* * *

Calvary knew that something was definitely up. The first sign had been Shawntriece's sister signing the twins out of school for the day. The second sign was the letter of job resignation that had just been emailed to him — it was from Shawntriece.

Did I move too fast? Is that the problem?

He picked up his phone to give Shawntriece a call, but he quickly realized that she had blocked his number — all of them. Business and personal. Then he stood up, intent on making his way to her home, hoping she was there so they could talk.

He was walking out of his office when he ran into his sister, Yolanda, with her hand poised midair as if she was about to knock on the now open door.

"Calvary. We need to talk."

He shook his head. He frowned. "Unless it's an emergency, I'm on my way out, sis. I have to find Shawntriece."

Yolanda's instincts told her that Shawntriece had, indeed, gotten her letter that day. This caused Yolanda to frown, too. "This is about Shawntriece, and trust me big brother, you're gonna want to hear what I have to say."

Calvary suddenly noticed the same look on Yolanda's face that she used to wear as a kid whenever she was guilty of something. The fine creases in his forehead became noticeable as he drew his eyebrows together. "What did you do, Landa?"

She was nervous now. "Well, you see… Um… Well, what had happened was… Well..."

"What did you do, sis?"

Yolanda took a deep breath and finally told her brother the whole story. After she'd had her say, she frowned at him and added, "I know it was mostly Tasha's idea, but I'm sorry for the role that I had in all this. I was wrong. I was just trying to protect you and Neek. I hope you can forgive me, Cal."

He let out a breath in a sigh. "I forgive you, sis. Now, I have to convince my baby that I'm completely innocent."

"I'll vouch for you, Calvary…you know that. Xavier and mama will, too. We all know what really happened."

The wheels in Calvary's brain were turning. He finally stroked his chin and said, "I'll keep that in mind. But I'm hoping that you won't have to."

"You have an idea… A way to make her understand?"

"Maybe."

* * *

It had taken a lot of energy — mental, emotional and spiritual — for Shawntriece to compose her letter of resignation and e-mail it to Calvary. She'd be lying if she said she hadn't been expecting him to try to reach out in some type of way in response to her quitting her job. That's why she wasn't surprised when her laptop sounded, notifying her that she'd received an email at her private email address — the one reserved for personal friends and family only.

Of course, it was from Calvary and the subject line of the message was: *Please DO NOT delete this. Please hear me out.*

Frowning, Shawntriece clicked on the message. She was expecting written text. However, the email was composed entirely of a video. She could tell from the video's preview that Calvary had recorded himself speaking. Part of her was inclined to play the video. However, just the thought of Calvary being a child predator caused her to move the entire message — video included — to the trash folder on her laptop's screen. Her heart wouldn't allow her to watch the video and listen to whatever he had to say.

It was a hard thing to do, but she forced herself to walk away from her computer. Her cell phone began ringing as she made her way to her living room sofa with the intention of lying down. She suspected it was Calvary calling again, so, she ignored the device.

She laid down on the sofa, curled herself up in the fetal position and had another good cry. *When will the pain end, Lord?*

The temptation was strong to blame God again, but Shawntriece refused to do that. Her spirit needed the Lord and she knew his love would be the only thing that would carry her through the emotional storm she was facing.

An hour later, she felt empty as she heard someone ringing her doorbell.

"It's me, boo… I know you're in there. I'm about to use my spare key and come in."

Shawntriece didn't even bother to open her eyes as her sister walked into her home, deactivated the security alarm and joined her in the living room.

"Oh, sweetie," RoShonda said in concern. "I just dropped the girls off at the bakery…they're with mama. I decided to come back over here and check on you since I called three times and you wouldn't answer your phone."

Shawntriece knew why her sister had done that. Her depression and despair had been so great right after the rape had happened that she'd contemplated suicide. Shawntriece finally summoned the energy to open her eyes a sliver. "I'm okay, Shonda. I just needed to rest. Calvary sent me a video gram through my email…I couldn't open it." She swallowed past the lump in her throat. "The sight of him made me sick to my stomach."

RoShonda frowned. "Now, I have no idea what he could possibly be saying in the video — since I suspect he doesn't know that you know about what happened at that school in Virginia — but you should probably listen to it, Shawny. Remember, before I left here to pick up the twins, you agreed to hear him out."

Shawntriece shook her head. "I can't, Shonda… I just can't do it."

"Do you want me to listen to it with you?"

"I can't."

"I'll listen to it *for* you then, honey. If it's something that I feel like you should know about, I'll let you know. Is that okay with you?"

Shawntriece pointed towards her study. "On my laptop…I deleted it. It's in the trash folder. Close the door so I don't have to hear it."

The video was almost ten minutes long. RoShonda was only thirty seconds in when she realized that Calvary definitely knew that her sister had found out about his secret. However, by the time she'd heard his message in its entirety, her heart was much lighter. She knew she had a good word to report to her sibling.

"He's innocent!" she shouted as she ran back into the living room. "You gotta hear him out, sis!"

Shawntriece narrowed her eyes at her sibling. "What?"

"He's innocent, girl. Just listen to the video…your honey bear explains everything, and he even has proof to back him up."

Shawntriece had a sliver of hope now. She knew her sister wouldn't lie to her like that. She finally sat up from where she'd been balled up on her sofa.

Grinning like a fool, RoShonda pressed the play button on the video to start it from the very beginning. "Here you go…listen."

Never in her life had Shawntriece cried tears of relief. She did that day as Calvary's hastily put together video came to a close.

Recorded from the sanctuary of his office at school, he explained how a fourteen-year old student had accused him of having sex with her because, infatuated with him, she was angry he wouldn't reciprocate on her advances. Fortunately for Calvary, the young woman had decided to talk to one of her friends about her plans to bring revenge on him. It turned out that the girl had undertaken her conversation in her baby brother's nursery. Without knowing it, the baby monitor had been left on. Bottom line, the mother found the footage and turned the video in to the authorities, thus, clearing Calvary's name. Calvary had even included a copy of the audio from the baby monitor as proof for Shawntriece to listen to.

RoShonda gave her sister a hug. Then she laughed. "See there, honey. I told you there had to have been a reason you didn't find any convictions when you did the background check. Your man is innocent."

When Shawntriece hopped off the sofa and began brushing her hair back from her face, trying to make herself look presentable, RoShonda wasn't at all surprised. She chuckled again and said, "That's right, go get yo' man, girl."

In less than five minutes, keys in hand, Shawntriece was flying out her front door, intent on making her way to Higher Ground Academy, intent on finding her Calvary. Turns out a drive wasn't necessary — at least not on her part. Calvary was pulling into her spacious triple driveway before she could make it to her car.

He knew — from the way she ran to him and threw her arms around him — that everything was alright. But a hug wasn't enough for Calvary. He had to lay claim to those luscious, full lips that he hadn't been sure he'd be able to kiss again.

"Oh, babe," Shawntriece said, almost a full minute later when they dragged their lips apart for some much-needed air. "I'm sorry that I was gonna cut you off like that."

He slowly turned his lips up in the smile that Shawntriece had come to find so darn sexy. "I guess that means I can ignore your resignation letter and that our wedding is still on?"

She grinned, too. "You better believe it, Calvary Powell."

Fifteen minutes later, as the couple sat cuddled up together on her sofa, Shawntriece leaned back against Calvary's broad chest and sighed in contentment. She couldn't believe that Tasha Parker had eavesdropped and run to Calvary telling him that she overheard her telling RoShonda that she wanted a marriage of convenience. And she also couldn't believe that Tasha had come up with the idea to mail the letter to her.

"What is that sigh about, babe?" Calvary asked.

Shawntriece smiled. "I just think it's amazing how everything Tasha did to try to break us up only drew us closer together. After everything that happened today, I wanna marry you right now, Calvary Powell."

"We can always go to the justice of the peace," he teased.

She laughed. "I know our wedding is only gonna be a small affair, but our little ladies would never forgive us if they don't get to be flower girls and lead me down the church aisle. It's only a couple of weeks from now…We can wait."

Calvary grinned. Yes, he could wait. He had a lifetime ahead of him to show Shawntriece every day just how much he loved her.

EPILOGUE

Sitting in his bedroom at two in the morning with only the display from the alarm clock on his nightstand providing illumination, Calvary lovingly looked down at his wife's sleeping figure. He found it hard to believe that a whole year had gone by since they'd exchanged their wedding vows. Shawntriece was asleep, but he suspected that she somehow realized he was staring at her, admiring her. Why? Because she suddenly turned over on her side and faced him. Eyes still closed, she yawned and stretched her arms. "Calvary," she said, her brain foggy.

He smiled as he began tracing the outline of her slightly rounded belly that bore the fruit of the love that they shared for each other.

"I'm right here, babe," he said, right after placing the softest of kisses on her belly button — the one that pregnancy had made more of an outtie than an innie.

"You okay, Bae?" she whispered.

"Yep. Just up thinking about how grateful I am for everything I got… You, our girls—," he placed a hand protectively over her stomach, "—and our son. Thank you for agreeing to marry me, babe. You don't know just how happy, how blessed I feel to have you as my wife."

Shawntriece smiled in her state of semi-sleep. She knew alright. Of course, she and Calvary had occasional disagreements, like any married couple did, but her man made it a point to remind her — at least two or three times a week — how special he thought she was.

"I'm the blessed one, Bae," she whispered as she drifted back into LaLa Land.

He grinned. It felt good to be loved by his sweetheart. As he laid back down beside her and wrapped his arms around her womanly softness, he had to admit that they were both blessed. They had each other and they had their God. There was no greater love. None.

Other Taretha Jones Books In The *True Love from God* Series

LOVING JASMINE
PAPERBACK ONLY $9.95

Item Code: TAJO005

Jasmine Washington is stunningly beautiful, saved and single. As an upwardly-mobile professional, her career is the main focus of her life. When she meets handsome ex-NBA player, Paul Bullock, she doesn't like him. She assumes he's a womanizer and an arrogant jerk. When they're thrown together on one of her job assignments, Jasmine begins to realize that Paul wasn't really the womanizer she'd believed him to be. The two have a mutual attraction and it doesn't take them long to fall in love. But will unholy indiscretions from her past, cause a deep hurt in their present? A hurt that threatens everything they've been blessed with from above.

FINDING FAITH
PAPERBACK ONLY $9.95

Item Code: TAJO006

Faith Johnson is beautiful, saved, and single. When she meets Minister-in-Training, Trayshawn Anderson, and he asks her to marry him, she's sure God has given her the desires of her heart through Trayshawn. But things aren't always as they seem and Faith soon realizes that Trayshawn was a gift from the devil himself. When ex-heavyweight boxing champ, Raymond Bullock, rescues Faith from a sticky situation, he can't help but fall in love with the kind-hearted, lovely girl. It doesn't take long for their love to become mutual. But is love enough to secure a happy-ever-after for the couple? Or will Raymond end up losing his Faith?

ROMANCING MONICA
PAPERBACK ONLY $9.95

Item Code: TAJO007

Monica Hall is a single, beautiful, saved sista who's got it going on. She has her very own nationally-syndicated radio talk show, and she has friends & family who love her. Despite all of that, deep down in her heart, she yearns for a soulmate. When her best friend gets engaged, Monica meets Olympic gold-medalist, Anthony Bullock. Anthony rubs Monica all the wrong ways. As luck would have it, she soon discovers that Anthony may not be as bad of a person as she'd thought he was. Anthony on the other hand...well he's smitten with Monica from the very beginning. When everything's said and done, will he be able to romance her and win her heart?

Firstman Publications   www.firstmanbooks.com

DATE:_____________

Firstman Publications, P.O. Box 14302, Greensboro NC 27415
Email: firstmanpublications@gmail.com

www.firstmanbooks.com

BILL TO

NAME____________________________ COMPANY____________________________
ADDRESS____________________________
CITY____________________________ ST________ ZIP________
Phone(______)____________ Fax(______)____________ E-Mail____________

SHIP TO

NAME____________________________ COMPANY____________________________
ADDRESS____________________________
CITY____________________________ ST________ ZIP________
Phone(______)____________ Fax(______)____________ E-Mail____________

Book Title	Item Code	How Many	Price Each	Total Price

☐ Money Order enclosed payable to Firstman Publications -OR-

Credit Card Number____________________________

Name on Card____________________________

Expiration Date____________ CVV Code____________

Signature____________________________

TOTAL AMOUNT	
SHIPPING: $3 for one book. $1 each additional book.	
SALES TAX: N.C. Add 7%	
GRAND TOTAL	